SUFFER SMOKE

Elena Díaz Björkquist

Authors Choice Press
San Jose New York Lincoln Shanghai

Suffer Smoke

Authors Choice Press
an imprint of iUniverse.com, Inc.

For information address:
iUniverse.com, Inc.
5220 S 16th, Ste. 200
Lincoln, NE 68512
www.iuniverse.com

Originally published by Arte Público Press

ISBN: 0-595-18357-3

Printed in the United States of America

ACKNOWLEDGMENTS

Muchismas gracias to *mis padres* Natividad *y* Valentine Herrera, *mi hermano*, Richard Herrera, *mis primos hermanos*, Carlos Todd *y* Tomás Todd, and all my other relatives and friends who shared their memories of Morenci. I owe a special thanks to my friends: Linda Feyder, for encouraging me to dig deeper and to Lee Reynolds and Rosalie Reynolds for their help in proofreading. Thank you also to the Anderson Valley Writer's Group for their helpful comments. To my husband, Kurt Björkquist—I couldn't have done it without you! Thank you for thirty-one years of love and support and your willingness the past four years to let the spirits of Morenci live with us. To Tata, Mamá Teresita, Granma Pepa (all three in heaven), and all those others of your generations—*les doy gracias* for your courage to leave your families and friends in Mexico and come to Morenci. Without you, none of these *cuentos* would exist.

For my great-grandmother,

Josefa Cruz Limón

and the legacy she left

to the children of Morenci.

CONTENTS

SUFFER SMOKE

PREFACE

I was born in Morenci in the mountains of southeastern Arizona, an isolated copper-mining town, as were my parents, aunts, and uncles, brothers, and most of my cousins. Most of the men who mined the copper were Mexican-Americans, descendents of the *Mexicanos* who were brought in from the mines of northern Mexico. Four generations of my family worked in the Morenci mine—from the time it was underground until it became an open pit—a pit so large, it swallowed the town whole.

Phelps Dodge Corporation, or P.D. as we called it, was the major employer. Except for a few businesses owned by individuals, people either worked in the mine or in the company's support services. Since P.D. owned the town, the mine, and the surrounding mountains, the company could do what it wanted. In the sixties, the company chose to expand the mine and Morenci was destroyed.

Thomas Wolfe said, "You can't go home again." This is especially true for us, the former residents of Morenci—not just because we've changed, but because our town no longer exists. In the end, P.D. won. P.D. bought people's homes and destroyed the town in a neverending quest for profit. The company built a new Morenci, but it's not the same. Phelps Dodge obliterated over ninety years of Morenci's history and culture. The new town is nothing like the old.

Morenci is now a ghost town, but not like Jerome, Arizona, where ruins of old houses dot the hills. Morenci is a spirit town. It lives in the memories of those who grew up there and it infiltrates our dreams. What is it about this town that continues to hold such power over us even after its demise? It's a question I ponder each time I awaken from a dream-

Morenci. Perhaps it's the spirits of people who were born there, the ones who worked in the mine until they died. No longer having a town to haunt—they haunt us, the survivors, by recreating Morenci in our dreams.

Some writers say they write to learn something about themselves. I agree. These *cuentos* were a voyage of self-discovery. Before I began writing, my dreams were haunted by Morenci almost every night, but as I committed more stories to paper, those dreams came with less frequency—I've survived the "suffer smoke."

Morenci lives in our memories. It lives in us—its children.

Elena Díaz Björkquist
Meadow Ridge
January 1995

JUST REWARDS

Juana wrung out the last sheet and sighed as she hung it up to dry next to the others billowing in the breeze. Finished at last. Each day it seemed to take longer to wash and starch the hospital linen. She surveyed her yard. A couple of clotheslines hung from the unpainted shack and led to the single tree growing in hard-packed ground. Other lines stretched in every direction from the house to posts standing like so many tall crosses in a graveyard. White sheets and pillowcases flapped over the lines, sounding like hundreds of geese on the wing.

On the hill below, Juana glimpsed other women going about their chores. Some hung out the wash, while others tended their gardens. Soon a few of them would head to the company store with their baskets to buy groceries. The joyful sound of children playing in the schoolyard at the very bottom of the hill drifted up to her. She thought of her grandson, David, playing with the other children and she smiled.

Juana turned to the metal wash tubs. A corrugated tin roof, stuck out from the side of the shack like an afterthought, sheltered them. She filled a chipped enamel basin with sudsy water from a tub and doused the smoldering fire beneath a heavy cast-iron cauldron. Earlier, she had boiled water and lye soap in the cauldron.

Drying her rough, chapped hands on her apron, Juana hurried over to the farthest line of sheets. With luck, she could bring in a load to iron before someone saw her and came over to gossip. The sheets were damp. Good—she would not have to sprinkle them. The hot Arizona sun dried everything quickly. Sometimes it seemed the linen started to dry as she hung it up.

She looked at her brown hands as she removed the clothes pins. They contrasted sharply against the brilliant bleached sheets. Once she had been so proud of her hands. People used to notice them and tell her how beautiful they were. *Don* Alfredo called them his winged brown sparrows. How he loved to study her hands. *Gracias a Dios*, he could not see them now. They were ugly—wrinkled and raw from scrubbing thousands of sheets all these years.

The four gold rings he had insisted on buying for her shined as brightly as the day he gave them to her—two on each hand. She remembered how he kissed each finger as he slipped a ring on it. "Beautiful rings to show off beautiful hands," he said. But no longer. Juana touched her face—it too felt as creased as her hands.

Had it been only nine years since *Don* Alfredo died in the mining accident? It seemed like an eternity. No, she must not think about it. She grabbed damp wrinkled sheets off the line and threw them into a worn wicker basket. Inside the coolness of the one-room house, Juana dropped the basket on the floor next to a round table. A blanket folded into several layers and covered by an old sheet padded the surface of the table. Two flat irons waited on the wood stove in preparation for the chore she detested.

Juana pulled out a sheet from the basket and spread it over the table. She folded a towel into a pad and took an iron off the stove. No need to check if it was hot enough. She could feel the heat in spite of the thick padding. Ironing had never been one of her favorite chores even before her husband's accident. How ironic she was now forced to do so much of it.

Don Alfredo and their only son, Tomás, both died in the accident. Her whole world collapsed around her as the tunnel had on them. Their poor bodies were so bruised and broken when they were dug out, the caskets had to be kept closed at the wake. Maybe that is why she could not stop thinking about them when she was alone. She had not had a chance to say a proper goodbye. She crossed herself and prayed to *la Virgen de Guadalupe* that her loved ones had not suffered.

The rest of the day dragged as Juana ironed the sheets in the basket and brought in others off the lines. She carried in wood and stoked the fire in the stove. It had to be hot enough to heat the irons. The work had a monotonous rhythm to it. First one hot iron slid over a sheet, smoothing out wrinkles until it cooled and no longer did its work. Back to the stove it went and it was the other iron's turn. The iron flew back and forth, guided by Juana's no longer beautiful hands.

By midafternoon, the sun beating down on the shack's corrugated tin roof and the fire burning in the wood stove turned the room into an oven. A breeze blowing in the yard whipped the sheets back and forth and Juana wished she could be outside. Instead, she removed her shoes and cotton stockings and tucked the hem of her long black skirt into her waistband to form loose pants around her legs. Sweat ran down her back and dampened her hair. She peered in the cracked dresser mirror and pinned her thick braids into a crown over her head. So much white among the black! The years of hard work were taking their toll.

If only for herself, she would not work so hard, but she had David to consider. If not for David, she would have no reason to live. *Pobrecito* David, so much misfortune to befall a young boy. His mother had died giving birth to him, then his father was killed in the accident.

Juana cursed the mining company. She blamed it for the deaths of her loved ones. If the doctor at the company hospital had tended Alicia properly, she would not have bled to death. If Alicia had been a Gringa, she would have gotten the best care. If *Don* Alfredo and Tomás had been Gringos, the company would have been more safety conscious and propped up the mining tunnels. How often had *Don* Alfredo complained about the inadequate supports? So many "ifs."

Juana was bitter. The company refused to pay death benefits for either her husband or son. It was fortunate *Don* Alfredo insisted on joining *el Beneficio Propio*, the local burial society. It had paid for their funerals. Otherwise, she would not have had the money to bury them. She cringed as she remembered the day she'd approached the hospital director. In spite of her limited English, she convinced him to hire her as a washerwoman. He was the same doctor who let Alicia die. Juana was angry and hated the man and what he represented, but she did it for David. It was the only way she could earn enough to support him.

The clock on the bureau chimed three times. *Por Dios*, David would be home soon and she was not finished with the ironing. The remaining sheets and pillowcases hung on the lines like the robes of papier-mâché *Santos* made in the Mexican village of her birth. She could bring them in later. They would have to be sprinkled before they could be ironed. Juana finished ironing the last sheet and placed it in a basket with the others. She released her skirt from the waistband and shook it out around her.

Preparing food for David was something Juana enjoyed doing almost as much as she relished watching him eat. He had a good appetite, just like his father and grandfather before him. They made food seem more delicious than it was— even a simple meal of beans and tortillas. Juana tried not to splurge on food. Every cent she could spare went into their California fund. When David graduated from high school seven years from now, she hoped to have enough saved to leave Morenci. David would not be a miner like her husband or son. She would not sacrifice her only grandson to the mine. David was smart—he could make something of himself with an education. No, David would not be a miner.

"Nana, I'm home." The screen door slammed behind him as ten-year-old David burst into the room.

Juana admired her grandson as he maneuvered around the crowded room toward her. He dumped his books on the table and hugged her as if he had not seen her in days. She inhaled the fresh scent of his clean blond hair and looked into his clear blue eyes before kissing first one smooth cheek then the other. His coloring always surprised her. It came from Alicia's side of the family. Otherwise, he looked so much like his father—it hurt to look at him.

"Did you learn anything new at school today, *m'ijo*?" Juana asked.

"Just the usual—math, English, and history. Science was really fun. I could do science all day. Do you want me to bring in the sheets?"

"Not right now. First we eat and then we go to the dump to see what we find. The sheets can wait." Juana served him a plate of freshly cooked beans with the *verdolagas* she had picked that morning. *Gracias a Dios* for providing plenty of greens on the surrounding hills. Between purslane and cactus, she always had fresh vegetables. She heated a flour tortilla on the stove, peeled it off, and flipped it onto David's plate.

David savored the beans as he shoveled them with tortilla chunks into his mouth. When they finished eating, David stacked the dirty dishes in the sink.

"Do you have homework?" asked Juana.

"No, Nana. I finished all my work at school today."

Juana took a kettle of boiling water from the stove and poured it over the dishes. "Let us leave these to soak while we go to the dump."

She put on her shoes and took the black- and gray-striped *rebozo* David held out for her. Wrapping one end over her head and chest, she flung the other across the opposite shoulder. At the small altar to *la Virgen de Guadalupe* near the door, they both paused and crossed themselves before going out for their daily scavenger hunt through the dump. David retrieved their walking sticks from the lean-to and handed one to Juana.

When *Don* Alfredo was alive, Juana never went to the dump or poked through other people's cast-off junk. In those days she lived in a spacious house and never imagined she would have to move to a shack next to the dump. Yet here she was. With each passing year, an evening excursion through the dump was the big adventure of her day. Sometimes she and David found something for their own use. Other times, it was something they could fix to sell—but more often, they found nothing of value.

David ran ahead, stopping now and again to poke his stick into interesting debris. He turned over a wooden crate to see what was underneath.

"Look, Nana, a doll." He picked it up and held it over his head so Juana could see.

"Good find, David! We can clean her up and I will crochet a dress for her. We can sell her for a quarter."

Juana overturned a box full of papers. It must be from the company administrative office, she thought as she nudged through it with her stick. Probably just scrap paper. She was about to move on when something caught her eye. A jab of the stick revealed a rectangular canvas bag. Juana picked it up, pulled open the drawstring around the top, and peeked inside. Her eyes grew wide, and a soft *"Dios mío"* escaped her lips. She yanked the bag closed and tucked it into the *rebozo* criss-crossing her breasts.

"David, hurry. Come. We must go." Juana raced toward the shack as if her feet had sprouted wings. There was so much to do.

Article from *The Copper Times*
dated Tuesday, October 28, 1924
Morenci, Arizona:

COMPANY PAYROLL MISSING!

Payday came and went without money for several hundred miners last Friday. For the first time in Taylor Dunne history, it failed to meet a payroll.

Rumors abound about why the miners were not paid. Requests to company officials for more information have been met with "no comment." However, an inside source has revealed that a cash bag with part of the payroll is missing.

Since officials refuse to make a statement, it is not known how much money was contained in the missing bag. It is speculated a substantial amount was lost, given the number of miners who were disappointed when their turn to be paid came and there was no money.

The double doors to Holy Cross Church flew open and parishioners streamed out. Clusters of people gathered in front of the church to catch up on the week's events in Morenci. They exchanged more news every Sunday after church than the town's newspaper printed every week.

A few individuals, however, were not pleased with this weekly ritual and complained regularly to *Padre* Miguel. They urged him to disperse the crowd after Mass. *Padre* Miguel nodded his head as if he agreed with them, but did nothing. The short, pudgy Spaniard in his brown Carmelite robes loved the after-Mass conversation as much as the members of his congregation. Every Sunday, he stripped off his vestments, slipped out the side door, and waited in front of the church as the last parishioners filed out. It was his custom to drift from group to group, grazing for news and expounding his opinion.

This Sunday, the missing money bag was the main topic of conversation. However, a few *señoras* surrounding the priest had another concern.

"*Doña* Rosalba, do you know where *Doña* Juana has gone?" *Señora* Dominguez asked Juana's next-door neighbor. "She missed Mass again today."

"No. I stopped by her house Tuesday and she was not home. There were sheets hanging on the clotheslines and when I peeked through the screen door—I saw dishes in the sink."

"Perhaps she is sick," *Padre* Miguel said. "She never misses Mass. You know how she loves to sing the solo during Holy Communion." Secretly, he had not missed Juana's off-key soprano.

"Something must be wrong, *Padre*," *Señorita* Castillo said. "Her grandson, David, hasn't been in school for a week."

"But her house looks as if she stepped out only for a little while," *Doña* Rosalba said.

"Maybe we should go check on her," the priest said.

"Pardon me, *Padre*. I could not help hearing about *Doña* Juana," *Señor* Tamayo said. He and his friends merged with the priest's group. "I know where she is. *Doña* Juana and David went to visit her aunt in *Tejas*."

"What aunt?" *Doña* Rosalba asked. "Juana does not have relatives. Besides she would not leave the hospital sheets hanging on the line and dirty dishes in the sink."

"But that is what she told me. She said, 'I go to the house of my *tía* in *Tejas*.' Do you think I would make up such a thing?"

"*Cálmese, Señor*." *Padre* Miguel patted the taller man's arm. "When did *Doña* Juana tell you this?"

Señor Tamayo pulled his beard. "Ah, yes, it was the day before I picked up Fernández's chickens in Duncan. That would be a week ago last Thursday. That is when she sent David for me."

"Why did she want you?" asked *Señorita* Castillo.

"It is as I have been telling you. She was going to *Tejas*."

Curiosity spread among other parishioners clustered around the church. After all, no one knew much about the missing money bag and they had already picked apart the more exciting theories of where it could be. The whole congregation merged with the group discussing Juana's mysterious disappearance.

"Did she send David just to tell you that?" *Padre* Miguel asked.

"No, of course not. She wanted me to drive her and David downtown to the train depot so she could take the train to *Tejas*. She gave me two dollars."

People on the edge of the crowd jostled the ones in front.

"What is this about *Doña* Juana?"

"*Doña* Juana is a penny pincher. She would never give anyone a dollar, much less two!"

The entire congregation talked at once. Speculation ran wild about why Juana might have gone to Texas. Finally, *Padre* Miguel climbed to the uppermost step in front of the church. He stretched his lips at the corners and blew a piercing whistle. Silence fell over the crowd.

"All right, everybody, let us solve this mystery logically," said the priest. He peered through his round, tortoise-shell glasses at his flock. "What do we know thus far?"

"Juana is missing," *Doña* Rosalba said.

"Just like the money bag," *Don* Martín said.

"She lives by the dump," *Don* Pablo said.

"Maybe the money bag was thrown out with the trash," *Don* Martín said.

"The dump!" *Don* Pablo yelled.

Two Articles from *The Copper Times*
dated Tuesday, November 4, 1924
Morenci, Arizona:

MOB DESCENDS ON DUMP

The Morenci Dump was the scene of hectic activity last Sunday as a large mob spearheaded by what appeared to be the entire congregation of Holy Cross Catholic Church searched for the missing Taylor Dunne money bag.

Apparently, a fellow parishioner, Juana Gutiérrez, had been missing for a week and a half. At first it was feared Mrs. Gutiérrez had met with foul play, but upon further investigation it was learned she and her grandson, David, age 10, left town of their own volition.

When someone remembered Juana lived next to the dump, the parishioners thought she might have found the money bag and left town. The congregation flocked to the dump pursued by their priest, Father Miguel. It was not clear if he were giving chase to stop or to join them.

Members of the Presbyterian Church were ending their service when they heard the commotion and joined the mob before Reverend Daniels could begin the closing hymn.

The ever-growing mob streamed past the Chinamen's quarters and were joined by several dozen Chinese, their queues flying behind them as they brought up the rear.

By the time the mob descended on the dump, it was estimated at least three-quarters of the town's population was involved. The scene at the dump site was astounding. Hundreds of people in their Sunday best were poking around in garbage. Not one area was left untouched. A few people brought shovels, but many others were rooting through the garbage with their bare hands.

No trace of the money bag was found, although some townspeople were looking well into the night.

MONEY BAG STILL MISSING

Taylor Dunne official Duane Lawrence, confronted by several reporters including a couple from the major newspapers in Tucson and Phoenix, finally released a statement about the corporation's missing money bag.

"We were unable to meet our payroll two weeks ago due to the disappearance of a bag full of cash. Preliminary investigation into the case has shown the money was not stolen. Sheriff's deputies are still conducting the investigation."

Bombarded by questions, Lawrence refused to comment on the speculation that local resident, Juana Gutiérrez, may have found the money bag at the dump and left town.

Sheriff Heath, up for reelection this year, announced in a news conference from the County Courthouse steps that he is doing everything in his power to solve the case soon. He also refused to comment about Juana Gutiérrez.

Juana stepped out of the passenger side of the realtor's car and smoothed the short skirt of her burgundy suit. What beautiful material, she thought. She straightened the pert cloche that covered her bobbed hair.

Reaching back into the car for her purse, she noticed how her hands, gloved in gray, resembled dove wings. *Don* Alfredo would be so proud.

"*Ven*, David," Juana said. She opened the rear door and David stepped out. He was wearing a brown tweed suit with knickers that revealed a pair of blue and red argyle socks matching a natty bowtie. Yes, *Don* Alfredo would be very proud.

"This is one of the finest homes we have listed in your price range. It's just a few blocks from the new University of California, so your grandson won't have far to go when he gets into college," Mr. Simmons, the realtor, said. With a sweeping gesture he pointed to a modest bungalow at the end of a long cement walk. "I think you'll find it's everything you asked for."

A spacious porch ran across the front of the house, and beyond it, Juana could see the glimmer of a huge picture window. The lawn was a plush emerald-green carpet. She could not resist stepping on it, and her shoes sank into the deep grass. Dew drops from the long blades spotted her silk stockings. What a difference from her parched yard in Morenci!

Juana took David's hand as she followed Mr. Simmons up the walk. Hibiscus and bougainvillea grew against the house. Such beautiful flowers did not grow in Morenci; California was indeed a tropical paradise. The realtor opened the front door and invited them to enter. Juana stepped over the

threshold and knew she was home at last. She nodded at Mr.
Simmons as she looked at the living room, but refrained from
commenting. Best not to let him know how much she liked it
because she had no intention of paying the asking price.

What space compared to the one-room house they had
lived in! Their old house was smaller than the living room. In
the kitchen, gleaming like a jewel, was a green and yellow
Wedgewood stove supported on four black legs. Juana opened
the oven door and peered inside. It was smaller than her old
wood-burning stove, but no matter. This one had gas piped in
and would not require copious amounts of wood to be chopped.
Under a window overlooking the back yard stood a granite
sink with two metal water taps.

"One for cold water and the other for hot." Mr. Simmons
turned on each faucet.

Running water in the house! Juana's attention turned to
an oak icebox at the end of a counter. Brass handles gleamed
against polished wood.

"You can have ice delivered right to your door," Mr. Simmons said. He opened a door and showed Juana the inside.
"See the pipe there? It allows the water to drain off when your
ice melts so your food won't get soggy."

A door led to a screened-in back porch, and David walked
out into the back yard. "Look, Nana! Plenty of room for a vegetable garden." He turned to the realtor and asked, "Where's
the outhouse?"

"There isn't one. This house has indoor plumbing. Come
on, I'll show you." Mr. Simmons led the way to a hallway and
threw open a door. "*Voilà!* You have a bathtub and a toilet."
He flushed the toilet and demonstrated the hot and cold spig-
ots in the claw-foot bathtub.

Mr. Simmons showed them the three bedrooms. Juana
strolled through them—one for David and one for her, plus a
spare. The smallest one was perfect for a sewing room. Yes,
this house would do. David could grow up here and not be
ashamed of his old grandmother. Soon enough he would go to

college and maybe become a doctor or a lawyer. She patted her leather handbag—plenty of money in the new bank account to buy this house and send him to U.C.L.A.

"Mr. Simmons." Juana turned to the realtor. "There are a few problems with this house that need fixing. I do not think it is worth what the owners ask for it. If they are willing to take less, I think it will do."

"But of course." The realtor rubbed his hands together, the chunky diamond on his pinky finger twinkled. "The Reynolds are very willing to negotiate. Come—let's go back to the office and write up your offer."

As they walked back to the car, Juana turned for a last look. Yes—this house would do. It would do very well.

THE HERSHEY BAR QUEEN

When she was a little girl, Reyna Lara was the same size as other children her age. As they grew up, however, the baby fat melted off the others but Reyna's did not. Instead, she gained more and more weight. At first, it was not her fault. Her parents thought their one and only child was perfect with black sausage curls and cheeks like large ripe peaches. They pinched her cheeks and plied her with *pan dulce*, cookies, and candy. "Sweets for our sweet queen," they would tell her.

By the time she was seven, Reyna was the size of three girls her age and the other children made fun of her, calling her names like "Reyna, the big fat *ballena*." Her only playmates were her cousins and they played with her because they were forced to by their parents. Reyna did not seem to care. Food was her main concern and as she grew bigger and bigger, she had to consume even greater quantities to fuel her immense bulk. She took to visiting her grandmother every evening because Nana served dinner later than her mother. Reyna could eat another full meal there and Nana was liberal with seconds and sometimes thirds. Reyna's four aunts and three uncles also lived nearby and she picked up extra meals and snacks at their homes.

There was an emptiness inside Reyna—a hollow feeling she interpreted as hunger, but no amount of food could fill it, no matter how much she stuffed herself. She ate more than her father; probably more than anyone else in town, except maybe for *Doña* Lupe. The last time that lady was seen outside her house, she could barely squeeze out a door. It was rumored that now she was so enormous, she could not get out of bed. All *Doña* Lupe did was eat, sleep, and read *True Confessions* magazines.

When Reyna was twelve-years old, she stood five feet seven inches tall in her bobby socks and weighed 350 pounds. She towered a foot or more over the other girls her age and older. Reyna was taller, not to mention wider, than most women in Morenci, including her mother. Boys her age had not yet undergone growth spurts like the girls, so next to them Reyna was gigantic.

Despite being so large, Reyna was extremely graceful. When she walked, her tiny feet skimmed the earth as if held up by her buoyant body. The other children teased that she looked like a balloon in the Macy's Thanksgiving Day Parade. Their parents thought so, too, but kept it to themselves unless they were chiding their children for eating too much candy. "Quit it or you'll look like a balloon in the Macy's parade!"

The harassment Reyna suffered from schoolmates grew so severe she took to ducking into the Taylor Dunne Mercantile Store every day after school so she would not have to walk home with them. Reyna strolled up and down aisles stacked high with cans and boxes of food. She wandered through the fresh-vegetable section and thought about what *Mamá* and Nana might be preparing for dinner. She envisioned *tacos, enchiladas, mole, chili verde, gorditas, frijoles, calabacita, burritos,* and dozens of other delicious Mexican dishes, and her empty stomach grumbled its complaint. Reyna took a huge sack lunch to school every day, but it was not enough to sustain her until dinner.

When she thought the other children had enough head start, Reyna went to the candy counter. By this time in her life, her parents were concerned about her weight and were afraid she would wind up like *Doña* Lupe, so they limited her intake of sweets. They allowed her to buy only one candy bar each day and Reyna was obedient. Of course her parents did not know about the extra meals she obtained from the relatives.

"What'll it be today, Reyna?" asked the clerk. "A plain Hershey or one with almonds?" Reyna always left the pleasure of deciding until the last moment. There was no rhyme or reason as to which one she chose. Some weeks she picked Hersheys with almonds five days in a row and other weeks she alternated them with plain Hersheys every other day. Regardless of which she chose, Reyna always took her chocolate treasure across the large Plaza parking lot to the foot of the grand staircase leading up to the new shopping center. She could have taken the short cut across the footbridge over the road, but avoided it with reason.

When she used to cross the two-way bridge, people coming toward her would have to retreat and wait until she crossed. There was no way that anyone, not even a small toddler could squeeze past Reyna. She filled the passageway from one side to the other. Her girth was such that she could not even turn around on the narrow bridge. One day she attempted it and got wedged in so tight she could not move. The old men who sat in front of the T.D. store buying and selling coupon books rushed to her rescue. They extricated her from this humiliating predicament by tugging and shoving until she popped out like the first pickle in a jar. She landed on the nearest elderly man, who was never the same after that. Meanwhile, the children gathered on both sides of the bridge laughed and taunted her.

"Reyna's a *ballena!*" they yelled.

"She's so big and fat she can't cross the bridge!"

"Reyna's so big, she could be the bridge!"

After that, Reyna never went on the footbridge again.

There was another short cut. It went under the bridge and across the road to a steep staircase behind the Royal Theater, but it was also a problem for Reyna. Nearly a hundred narrow steps led to the top with only one place to rest halfway up. There was no shade where she could stop to eat her Hershey bar. The only time she had gone that route, Reyna thought she would die before she reached the upper level.

So Reyna was forced to take the grand staircase, although it was the longer route to her house. The WPA had built the staircase, during the Depression and it was grand indeed. Two sixty-foot tall cypress trees flanked it at the bottom and the wide stairs meandered uphill as if leading to a mansion. Her grandfather had helped lay the steps and walls enclosing the staircase, and Reyna always remembered him when she touched the stones worn smooth by thirty years of use.

Reyna's daily ritual was to sit on the wall shaded by the nearest tree and pull off the Hershey bar's brown outer wrapper. She sniffed it with delight, anticipating the taste of warm chocolate. The candy was usually melted, so she licked it off the foil wrapper. This was the way she liked it best, and since it was the only candy bar she could have, she savored every smidgen of chocolate her tongue lapped off the waxy white lining.

When every trace of chocolate had vanished, she crumbled the wrappers and tossed them under the cypress where they joined an ever-growing pile. Then Reyna commenced to climb the grand staircase, feeling like a queen. She paused now and again to rest on the stone wall and gaze down at the cars in the lot below. Some days, if she were lucky, she spotted one of her uncle's cars and went back down the stairs no matter how far up she was. She sat in the car and waited until its owner came out and drove her home. If she were not so lucky—which was more often the case, she climbed two more sets of stairs behind the post office and a large hill before she reached home.

On the day that would change the course of her life forever, Reyna saw Beto Cisneros sitting on the wall near the top of the stairs. He was sixteen-years old and in tenth grade. He would have been in eleventh grade if he had not flunked fifth. Normally, he did not bother glancing her way, much less speak to her, but on this day he surprised Reyna.

"Would you like a Hershey?" Beto asked. He held it out to her but pulled it back when she reached for it. "No. First I want to show you something." He grabbed her hand and pulled her toward the ivy-covered wall next to the power and light building.

Reyna was not sure what was happening so she locked her legs in place and yanked Beto toward her. He bounced off her body and plopped on the ground.

"It's okay, Reyna." Beto got up and offered his hand to her. "I just want to show you my secret hiding place. Come on."

Someone offering to share a secret hiding place, his hand, and a Hershey? No one in Morenci outside her family ever showed such kindness to Reyna. She went with him.

Beto led her up an ivy-covered path alongside the retaining wall. In all the times Reyna passed by here she never noticed the overgrown path. Halfway to the top of the forty-five-foot high wall, Beto stopped.

"Let's go in here." He pushed his way through overhanging ivy onto a four-foot wide ledge jutting out from the wall. Originally intended by the builders as a planter to break the expanse of rock wall, it once contained flowers, but now a jungle of ivy made the ledge invisible to passersby below. A shiver of anticipation went through Reyna as she joined Beto. Two Hersheys in one day!

"Sit." Beto pulled her onto the cushion of cool leaves next to him. "No one can see us here. This is my secret place. Nobody else knows about it so swear you won't tell anyone, not even your mother."

"I swear not to tell," Reyna said. Who would she tell? She had no friends, no one with whom she could share such an important secret.

"You have to do more than swear," Beto said. "You have to seal your oath."

"Seal my oath?" Reyna smelled the chocolate sweetness of the melted candy bar as Beto wafted it under her nose. A Hershey with almonds! Reyna licked her lips and her tongue encountered a smear of chocolate from the candy she had eaten only minutes before. She swiped it off with her tongue and its taste made her hunger for more. She reached out for the Hershey, craving it as if it were the last one on earth.

"No," said Beto. "First we seal the oath. We're going to form a secret club. I'm the leader and you'll do everything I say from now on."

"Okay. Fine," Reyna said. She eyed the Hershey in Beto's hand and hoped he would let her have it before it melted further. Reyna liked it melted on the outside but preferred the inside to be solid enough to get her teeth into it.

"Lay down and close your eyes." Beto pointed to the bed of ivy. Reyna obeyed him, but when she felt her dress slide up, her eyes flew open. "What are you doing?" She struggled to sit up.

"I'm not going to hurt you," Beto said. He nudged her back down. "This is what friends in our club do when they like each other. Close your eyes and relax. You don't have to do anything else."

Friends? Like each other? Not since she was a little girl had anyone offered to be her friend, much less say they liked her. Reyna lay back down—her eyes squeezed shut. She felt Beto slip off her underpants and climb on top of her. Suddenly, something poked her down there in that place her *mamá* had told her not to touch except when she wiped after peeing.

"Oomph!" Reyna's eyes popped open. Something was now inside her pee place and Beto bucked up and down like one of the cowboys Reyna saw riding the bulls at the rodeo.

"Ahh!" Beto grimaced as if something exploded inside him. His body went slack and he lay on her for a few minutes before rolling off and pulling up his jeans.

"That's it," he said. "Your oath is sealed. Here's the Hershey and your *chones*. Remember you can't tell anyone about this place or what we do in our secret club." He crawled through the leafy undergrowth back to the path.

Reyna sat up with her tent-sized panties in one hand and the Hershey in the other. She threw down the panties and ripped open the candy bar. Reyna's teeth scraped the entire gooey mess into her mouth. The delectable chocolate melted on her tongue and oozed down her throat.

There was something strange about what happened with Beto, but Reyna did not know what. It couldn't be wrong, could it? Beto was her friend and he said he liked her. Reyna chomped the almonds and twin streams of chocolate sluiced down either side of her mouth. At the same time, she became aware of a sticky wetness between her legs. She took a hanky out of her pocket and wiped herself. The handkerchief looked like someone with a bad cold had blown his nose in it. There was a tinge of blood running through the mucus. Had Beto broken something down there? Maybe she'd ask her mother when she got home. But no, she couldn't do that. She had promised Beto. Reyna stuffed the hanky in the ivy, put on her panties, and went home.

A couple of days later, Beto was again waiting at the staircase. He flashed the Hershey at her and led the way up the path. Without his help, Reyna found it difficult to maneuver her bulk up the steep slope. By the time she reached the ledge, she was panting.

"Take them off and lay down," Beto said. "I'll give you the Hershey when we're done sealing the oath." He mounted her and repeated what he had done earlier, except he did not take as long. "Remember this is our secret—don't you tell." He handed her the Hershey and left.

Reyna ate the candy with gusto, licking the wrapping and her fingers to get every last bit of chocolate. When she wiped herself this time there was no blood on the handkerchief. She wadded it up and stuck it in the ivy. Maybe she'd better carry Kleenex. Her mother might get suspicious about too many lost hankies.

For the next month, Reyna counted on getting an extra Hershey two or three times a week. Then one day she found

Matt Sandoval instead of Beto waiting for her on the stair-case. He flaunted two Hersheys.

"I'm in the club," he said. He turned and went up the ivy-covered trail. Reyna trudged behind him. More chocolate and a new friend!

In the weeks that followed, Sammy García, Tony Moreno, Andres Solano, and Martín Hernández had all joined the club. By the end of the year, Reyna had many more new friends and had gained twenty-five pounds.

By the time she was in eleventh grade, Reyna weighed 439 pounds. The young men in Morenci called her the "Her-shey Bar Queen" behind her back. When she was fifteen, her Aunt Tilly, who was seven years older, told her about sex. So now Reyna knew what the boys did to her on the ivy leaves was wrong. Every Saturday, when she dutifully waited in line to confess her sins, she thought about telling Father O'Hara. But how could she betray her friends? The boys were her only friends. The girls hated her. They made snide remarks about her weight and Reyna had had several fights in the girl's bathroom at school. Her bulk was an advantage and each scuffle ended with Reyna sitting on her antagonist. Nowadays no girl dared confront her, but Reyna still heard them whis-pering about her.

By now Reyna was a mother confessor to most of the boys. They sought her out not just for sex but as someone they entrusted with their joys and tribulations. They called her "Big Reyna" and felt comforted when she hugged them to her mountainous bosom. Reyna was a good listener and only offered advice when they asked for it. She did not condemn or criticize and was quick to offer encouragement. The boys made her feel needed. No, there was no way she could tell the priest about them and the Hershey Club.

Sometimes she felt guilty about holding back something she knew was a sin—especially on Sundays when she received Holy Communion. She was afraid that one day the Host would burn through her tongue as it dissolved. It would be God's way of punishing her for not confessing all her sins. Reyna was not even sure if she were committing a venial sin or a mortal one since the nuns had never mentioned anything about sex in catechism. She prayed it was the lesser one.

Toward the end of the school year, students prepared for the Junior Prom. When Mrs. Ames, the school secretary, posted the nominee list for king and queen on the bulletin board outside the office, Reyna was thrilled to discover her name. Her Hershey boys had come through! She had never been to a dance or even had a date. Now she was not only going to the prom, the biggest formal dance of the year, but the prom committee had nominated her for queen. That was all she could think about day and night in school and at home. In Home Economics, she forgot to take her cake out of the oven and the whole school was evacuated when smoke set off the fire alarm. Homework went unfinished. Teachers' questions she had not heard and could not have answered anyway, interrupted her daydreaming in class.

Her mother sewed all of Reyna's clothes since there were no store-bought dresses in her size. While other young women went to Safford to try on and purchase their gowns, Reyna and *Señora* Lara went to study the designs. In the end, they combined various styles and purchased yards of expensive satin, ribbons, and lace. *Señora* Lara spent hours sewing a gown fit for a queen. Reyna went on a diet, limiting herself to meals at home. She squirreled away Hershey bars from her assignations with the young men. The treasure house of chocolate she was hoarding tempted her to indulge, but Reyna disciplined herself. By the time she figured out she could exchange her favors for the promise of votes for prom queen instead of candy, the collection of Hersheys cached in the ivy was more than adequate for a super binge after the prom.

The night of the prom arrived and Harold Pankovich, who had been nominated for king, came for Reyna in his father's GMC pickup. Harold stood a foot shorter than she did and weighed about 110 pounds in his rented tux and black high-top basketball shoes. He had a reputation for being the most obnoxious person in all of Morenci High School history, but he was Reyna's friend and she overlooked his idiosyncrasies. When Harold saw Reyna in her strapless evening gown, he almost dropped the gardenia corsage he was holding.

"Wow! You look fantastic!" he said. He stood on tiptoes and attempted to pin the corsage on the layers of ruffles adorning her décolletage.

Señora Lara, who had been admiring the product of her handiwork, came to his assistance when she noticed Harold's fumbling fingers brushing the tops of Reyna's breasts. *Señor* Lara brought out his Polaroid camera and took a series of black and white photos of Reyna by herself and with Harold. As it turned out later, he was grateful he had.

Reyna and Harold entered the school gym and stopped to admire the tropical jungle decor. A momentary silence greeted them as everyone turned to stare at them. They walked to the table reserved for the royal nominees, unaware of the snickering and whispering they left behind them. The music started and boy after boy came to Reyna's table to reserve a dance with her. It was a perfect evening as far as Reyna was concerned. Her dance card was full and she basked in all the attention she received. She felt like she was already the prom queen.

During an intermission, Reyna went to the bathroom in the girls' locker room. She was in the large stall at the far end struggling with the unfamiliar garter belt and stockings when she heard a girl in the next stall mention her name.

"Did you see Big Reyna?" asked the girl. Reyna recognized Sharon Martínez's voice. "She looks like a wedding cake in that grotesque dress."

"Yeah, a wedding cake for a giant," said another girl. This one sounded like Priscilla Ayala. Both girls giggled. "It must have taken fifty yards of material to make her gown."

"A strapless gown...can you imagine? Every time she went out to dance, I thought her boobs would pop out. They must be the size of watermelons!" said Sharon. "If I were that fat, I'd be too embarrassed to leave my house."

Reyna grappled with the garter belt. Damn! Maybe it was supposed to go on over the panties not under. Yards of satin and lace ruffles impeded her attempts to fasten the stockings. Her face flushed. A wedding cake? Watermelon breasts? But Harold said she looked fantastic ... and the boys had all signed her dance card.

"She has no shame," said Priscilla. "She was flaunting her boobs at all the guys who danced with her."

"What do you expect from someone who's slept with every guy in the school for Hershey bars?" said Sharon.

"She's going to get hers tonight," said Priscilla. "I bet she really believes she's going to get crowned tonight." Both young women laughed and flushed their toilets simultaneously.

"When we counted the votes today, the Hershey Bar Queen had just one vote—hers!" said Sharon. "I can hardly wait to see her face when Sal announces the last runner-up and hands her a Hershey bar in front of the whole school." The girls' laughter echoed off the metal lockers.

Hot tears sprang to Reyna's eyes and mascara flowed down her rouged cheeks. She wiped the tears, smearing her face red and black like the school colors. Wait a minute, how did the girls know about the Hershey Club? The boys had to have told them. Reyna felt a pain in her heart as if a bolt of lightning had ripped through it. How could they? It was supposed to be a secret. All these years, she had kept her promise. Why hadn't they? Out of the hurt, a deep rage exploded. She clenched her fists and plunged out of the stall, ripping the locked door off its hinges.

In the mirror, Sharon and Priscilla glimpsed a bulk of white racing toward them—Reyna snorting like an enraged bull. The young women were so scared, they forgot to run. Reyna grabbed each one by their fancy hairdos and shook them like rag dolls. She flung their bodies into the toilet stalls.

Turning to leave, Reyna saw herself in the mirror. What a mess! Her curls, which had been piled high in an upswept hairdo, tumbled around her head like worms with hairpins stuck in them. Mascara mingled with rouge and flowed down her huge cheeks like lava from a volcano. For the first time in her life, Reyna saw herself as others saw her. Her fist pounded her reflection, splintering the mirror. Blood spurted out of her wounded hand and spilled onto the delicate lace of her dress. Intense hatred overcame her—hatred of the Hershey boys and of herself.

Reyna stormed out of the bathroom and into the gym, pushing aside anyone who got in her way. One shove from Reyna was enough to topple even Buzz Owens, the biggest football player on the team. Harold approached her and Reyna ran right over him like a locomotive. As Reyna made her way to the exit, she pulled down crepe-paper streamers and balloons. The cardboard murals of exotic jungles painted by the art classes crashed to the floor. A path of devastation lay in Reyna's wake. Teachers and students alike were so stunned they didn't even try to stop her.

Anger and hatred fueled Reyna as she tackled the 357 steps that led up from the high school to the plaza. Usually it took her forever to climb this steep staircase because she could not go more than ten or twelve stairs without stopping to rest. But this night, she flew over three and sometimes four steps at a time. At first Reyna did not know where she was going, but when she found herself at the foot of the grand staircase, she knew.

In the darkness, Reyna crawled onto the ivy-covered ledge and dug in the leaves for her cache of Hershey bars. She stuffed candy into her mouth as fast as she could get the wrappers off. Her jaws chewed the mass of hard chocolate—plain Hersheys and Hersheys with almonds—all mixed. Chocolate streamed down her chin and joined the other stains on her ruined gown. Bar after bar went into her cavernous mouth, but none of them brought the comfort she was seeking.

An almond stuck in her throat and Reyna tried to cough. She was choking. Desperate to breathe, she jumped up and the snaps on her garter belt broke. The belt slipped to her ankles, tripping her. Reyna reached out to grab the ivy to steady herself but she was facing the wrong way. Her hands closed on air. The tremendous weight of her upper body plunged her headfirst off the ledge into the ivy leaves below.

The townspeople organized a search party for Reyna that same night, but her body was not found until the next morning. Her parents were in shock. *Señora* Lara took to her bed clutching a tear-streaked snapshot of Reyna in her prom dress. *Señor* Lara was so distraught, his brother had to drive him to the mortuary in Clifton to arrange the funeral. Mr. Morrison informed them there were no caskets large enough for Reyna's body. He hated to do so because the markup on caskets was where he made most of his money. Reluctantly, he told them to ask *Don* Simón to custom-build a coffin. *Don* Simón was the former coffin maker who had been forced to retire when people preferred the fancy manufactured caskets to his wooden ones. It took him four days to build a specially reinforced coffin out of oak. Pine would have splintered under Reyna's immense weight.

On the day of the funeral, Holy Cross Church overflowed with family and parishioners and the entire population of Morenci High School—boys, girls, and teachers. Reyna's uncles had refused to carry the coffin because of their bad backs so *Señor* Lara invited the football team to be pallbearers. It took the whole first string plus one—six on each side—to carry Reyna's coffin down the church's main aisle. Father O'Hara spoke about Reyna and how much she had suffered in her short life but was now finally at peace. Girls sobbed into their hankies, feeling guilty about never having befriended her. Boys had lumps in their throats and felt guilty about having taken advantage of her.

When the funeral mass was over, the football team hoisted the coffin onto their shoulders again and trudged down the aisle. Outside the church, just before the steps, Buzz Owens slipped on what later turned out to be a melted Hershey bar— plain with no almonds. He tried to regain his balance but the coffin weighed him down and he stumbled into Larry Rodríguez, who fell onto Jorge Gutiérrez, who knocked over Salvador Tamayo, the heavy coffin crashing over all of them. It smashed into Beto Cisneros' groin and the blow was such that he was never able to father any children. The coffin slid down the stairs and knocked over several other young men who did not get out of the way fast enough. By the time Reyna's coffin came to a rest at the foot of the stairs, it had managed to injure over twenty young men. Each of the football players had broken something—an arm, a leg, a wrist, an ankle. It was a good thing the football season was over; otherwise Morenci could not have fielded a team that year.

Reyna's funeral turned into a shambles of broken bodies and screaming girls. When her uncles went to put the lid back on the coffin, they noticed Reyna had an angelic smile. It struck them as strange because when Reyna's casket lay open at the Rosary the night before, she was not smiling. With much effort, the older men of the parish loaded the huge coffin into the hearse and Reyna was finally laid to rest in the cemetery next to the smelter.

As far as the young men of Morenci were concerned, however, Reyna's spirit was never laid to rest. Those who went past the ivy-covered stone wall, where they had exchanged Hershey bars for Reyna's favors, heard the leaves rustle as if someone were tossing and turning on the ledge above. They caught a faint scent of chocolate as if someone were eating a Hershey bar next to them. Soon they sought other ways to get to the post office, although the grand staircase was the most direct route from the high school. Several years later when T.D. tore down Morenci for the ever-expanding copper mine, men who did not go to school in Morenci and did not know about Reyna had to smash the stone wall. The local young men refused to go near it.

Years later, when dynamite blasts obliterated Morenci and only the rocky levels of the open pit mine marked where the town once stood—workers reported there was a certain spot on a certain level where they heard leaves rustling and smelled chocolate. The young men who had known Reyna shivered every time they heard about it. They were destined never to forget Reyna, the Hershey Bar Queen.

THE ARIZONA CAFÉ

Marta Garcia admired the way her husband, Pedro, handled their new Nash sedan. As it slowed down to enter the small Arizona town, she noticed him glancing in large store windows to steal glimpses of the car. How proud he is of it, she thought. She didn't blame him—his first new car and it had taken fifteen years to buy it. He had started saving for the down payment when he got a job at the copper mine in Morenci, but things kept coming up—their wedding, the two children, and the war.

The war had changed Pedro. Before he went overseas, he was content with their lives. Now everything seemed to set him off. Marta grimaced as she remembered Pedro's argument this afternoon with his older brother, Juan. Pedro worshipped his brother and usually respected his opinion, but they had argued today about the union that the Chicano miners were starting. Pedro was thinking of joining it and Juan had warned that it might cost him his job. The other three brothers had sided with Juan. Marta had been counting on her brother-in-law to change Pedro's mind, but Juan only made him angrier and more determined to join the union. Pedro almost came to blows with his brother and stomped out of the wedding *fiesta* before the dance. She had gathered up their two children and joined him in the car. Now they were headed home to Morenci.

Why did Pedro want to rock the boat? Why couldn't he just accept things the way they were? He earned enough to feed and clothe them and even provide extras like this new car. Maybe it wasn't as much as the Gringos earned, but Chicanos had never earned as much as they did. That's just the way things were in Morenci.

Marta was scared Pedro would get into trouble. Her father had told her about a strike in 1903, the first time a miner's union had been organized. The leaders had been arrested and sent to the penitentiary in Yuma. Some of them were later deported. The union didn't last and not much changed in the mine.

Lose his job—jail? Marta felt her stomach lurch and closed her eyes. *Por favor, Madrecita de Dios,* don't let Pedro join the union. She hadn't been this afraid for her husband since the day she received the telegram saying he'd been wounded in action. Shrapnel in his head—surgery—a metal plate. Maybe that's what was making him act this way. She peered at his profile. Pedro sensed her looking at him and flashed his big-toothed smile. Marta smiled back. No, he wasn't crazy. She wished she could make him understand how she felt.

"*Mami,* Luis hit me!" Rosa, their five-year-old daughter, cried out from the back seat.

"*Niños,* stop that. Settle down." Marta turned and ordered the children to sit farther apart from each other.

"They're probably hungry. I could use a cup of coffee and a couple of burgers. How about you?"

Without waiting for an answer, Pedro pulled up into a gravel parking lot and came to a stop in front of a weather-beaten café. A sign in its dirty window proclaimed it open.

"Are you sure you want to stop here?" Marta placed her hand on Pedro's arm. "We're not that far from home. I can fix us something when we get there."

"We have the money, Marta. *Está bien.* This place doesn't look expensive."

"*Papi,* I'm hungry. I wanna eat a hamburger." Rosa, jumped up from the back seat.

Three-year-old Luis took up the cry. "I wanna burger! I wanna burger!"

"See, Marta, the children are hungry, too. We can't wait another hour. Let's eat here, rest a bit, then head for home."

"It's not the money I'm worried about. Don't you remember the stories we've heard about this town? The children and I can wait till we get home." Marta shook her head, her brow furrowed.

"No, *Papi*. I can't wait. I'm hungry now. Let's go eat burgers and french fries, and I wanna big chocolate milk shake, too," Rosa said.

"I wanna burgers and fries," Luis said.

"The children can't wait and neither can I. We'll eat here." Pedro got out of the car and opened the back door for Rosa and Luis. He picked up Luis and took Rosa by the hand.

"Pedro, I don't feel right about this. Remember what happened to José Romero in this town?" Marta didn't want to repeat the story in front of the children. Poor José—he'd been beaten so badly, he was hospitalized. Reluctantly, she climbed out of the car and closed the door.

"Stop worrying, *vieja*. That was in a bar and he was by himself. We're a family. This café is a bit run-down, but it looks like a family place. Let's go in." He nudged her forward so she was forced to open the screen door and enter. Her family followed her into the café's dim interior.

The diner looked no better on the inside than it had from the outside. A layer of grime coated the black and white tile floor. Marta wondered how anyone could stand to look at such a filthy floor and not mop it. The smell of rancid grease assailed her nostrils.

Clustered in the center of the room were four red Formica and chrome tables with red leatherette chairs. A few of the chairs' seats were split and sported patches of black electrical tape. The tape was peeling away in places, disgorging gray cotton stuffing. Matching booths in the same dilapidated condition were arrayed along the window wall. Each table held a chrome napkin dispenser, a salt and pepper shaker, and on the wall above, a record selector for the jukebox.

In a corner was the huge, brightly lit jukebox. Rosa let go of her father's hand and ran to it. "Look, *Papi, música.* Can we play the record box? *¿Por favor?*"

Marta retrieved the little girl and led her back to one of the booths. "No, *niña.* Sit down for now. Later we can see about music."

Pedro joined them at the table with Luis. The murmur of voices in the kitchen and the buzzing of flies battering themselves against the screen door were the only sounds.

Marta felt out of place in the dingy café. She was wearing her best dress, the pearls Pedro had brought her from Japan, and a new hat. She looked at Pedro in his double-breasted suit, and the children in the new clothes she had bought them for his cousin's wedding. They didn't belong in this greasy spoon.

Marta became uneasy as they waited. The longer they sat, listening to the droning flies, the more fearful she became. Her dread increased when she heard the word "Mexicans" whispered behind the kitchen door. She felt a rush of blood to her head and fanned herself with her white gloves.

What if a waitress didn't come? She hoped Pedro wouldn't get angry. Since the war, he had become too outspoken about situations like this. It was as if being under fire had given him courage to stand up for his rights. In one respect that was good, but in another it could cause problems, especially if he lost his temper.

"*Mami,*" Rosa asked, "can we have *música?*"

"*¡Música! ¡Música!*" Luis clapped his hands excitedly and swayed rhythmically as if already hearing music.

Pedro put a dime in the selector and showed the children which button to punch. The jukebox responded with the mellow voice of Frank Sinatra singing "Estrellita." Suddenly a door banged against a wall and a woman in a pink uniform and white apron burst out of the kitchen.

"What are you people doing here?" she screamed. She pointed to the wall on her left. "Can't you read?"

Marta and her family turned to look where the woman pointed. Tacked on the wall behind the greasy countertop was a hand-lettered sign. Tattered and faded, it looked as if it had hung there since the café was built.

"You probably can't. I'll read it for you: No Dogs or Mexicans Served Here. That means y'all. We don't want your kind here. Git out!"

Marta looked at Pedro. He was staring at his fists. She wished he had listened to her. The children trembled and started to cry. *Madre de Dios, por favor* don't let Pedro lose control. She could tell his reflexes were geared to fight. Months of trudging through jungles in the Pacific islands, ever alert for enemy attack, had prepared him to react in only one way. She watched him clench and unclench his fists.

"Didn't you hear me? We don't serve your kind here. Get out or I'll call the law down on you for loitering."

Marta was terrified. They had to get out of here before Pedro blew. She reached for Pedro's arm. A short fat man came out of the kitchen. His hairy belly peeked out between his greasy apron and graying T-shirt. "Can't you understand plain English?" he said. "She told you to git. So scram. Vamoose! *Adiós, amigos*." He signaled to the door with his thumb.

Pedro shook off Marta's hand and smashed his fist on the table, knocking the salt and pepper shakers to the floor. A hush fell over the room and no one moved. The only sound Marta heard was the pounding of her heart. She closed her eyes; her stomach churned. She envisioned a fight—the police coming—Pedro in jail. *Por favor, Dios, no.*

"Come on, *niños*, let's go. This is not a very nice place." Pedro's voice was calm. He picked up Luis and helped Rosa out of the booth.

Marta slid out behind her daughter and thanked God for keeping Pedro's anger in check. She slipped her hand firmly under Pedro's arm and tugged him towards the door.

"*Papi*, why are we going?" Rosa cried.

"I don't wanna go, I wanna eat." Luis struggled in his father's arms.

"Shh, *niños!*" Marta sent a silent prayer to *la Virgen de Guadalupe* that Pedro would continue to hold his temper. They had to get out of this miserable place before anything else happened.

"It's O.K., Marta." Pedro patted her hand and turned to the waitress. "Lady, put that sign on the door—then people can see what kind of place this is."

Pedro handed Luis to Marta and picked up Rosa. He walked out of the café with his head high. Marta followed him and the screen door slammed shut behind them.

The waitress screamed through the door, "You dirty greaser! Who the hell do you think you are? Don't ever come in here again."

Marta saw Pedro clenching his teeth as if trying to hold back his anger. His actions were slow and precise as he helped his family into the car. He got in and backed the car out of the parking lot.

"Why was the lady yelling at us?" asked Rosa. She popped up behind the front seat. Marta looked at Pedro and raised an eyebrow.

"Sit down and hush, Rosa. We have another hour to go before we're home."

"But why, *Papi?* Why couldn't we eat there?"

Marta turned around and said, "Listen to your father, *niña. Siéntate y cállate.*" Her cheeks were hot, but inside she felt cold.

Rosa plopped down on the seat next to Luis, crossed her arms across her chest, and pouted. Luis reached over and tickled her under the ribs. At first Rosa ignored him, but the stimulation was too much. She grinned and exploded into uncontrollable giggles. In retaliation, she tickled Luis. The children's laughter filled the back seat.

Pedro turned on the car radio and whispered to Marta. "How can we answer our children when we don't know why?

Why do Gringos treat us this way?" His large work-gnarled hands gripped the steering wheel. "Why do they hate us?"

"*Cálmate*, Pedro." Marta caressed one of his hands. "It's been this way all our lives." But did it have to be? It pained her not to have an answer for her children.

"It doesn't have to be this way." Pedro slapped the wheel. "Dammit! I'm a veteran. I fought for this country. Why can't I eat where I want?"

Marta felt like someone was squeezing her heart. Pedro wasn't just a veteran—he was a decorated hero. He had almost died saving two Gringos. For his bravery, he was awarded a Purple Heart and a Bronze Star. Why shouldn't he eat where he wanted?

"I'm not taking it anymore. For the sake of our children— I don't want them to grow up like we did," he said.

How many times had she gone through a similar experience? Each time it seemed to eat away at her a little more and left her feeling hollow—as if she were not a person. Afterwards, she always buried the incidents deep within her, not wanting to dwell on them. After all, that's how things were. But did they have to be that way forever? Maybe Pedro was right. Marta didn't want her children to feel like that. It made her angry they'd had to experience it today. And it would continue to happen unless... unless what?

"You're right. I want it to be different for our kids." Marta wiped her tears away with the gloves and stared out the window.

"Things won't change unless we make an effort. That's why I want to join the union. We can fight for our rights at work. When the company sees they can't intimidate us any more, the other changes will come."

Marta gazed at the landscape as the car sped past cactus and sagebrush—her eyes yearning for flowers, not this dreary unchanging desert. Suddenly, the sky and clouds in the east grew brilliant pink, then magenta. The drab desert took on the bright colors and in the distance the mountains turned a deep purple. Marta looked back at the sun setting in glorious shades of red. The mountains where the sun was sinking were black, but ahead the land basked in a rosy glow.

"Then go ahead—join the union," she said.

SUFFER SMOKE

It begins with a tickle in the back of my throat. I pull the sheet up over my head. Dear God, please don't let it come tonight. But the tickle turns to a wheeze as I catch a faint whiff of sulfur.

I close my eyes and picture the sulfur smoke billowing out of the smokestack down at the smelter. When it's released, the sulfur smoke almost always comes to Morenci and fills our bowl-shaped town to its topmost hill.

I imagine it creeping up the mountains to Morenci. "Suffer smoke." That's what my little cousin Tomí thinks we call it—and "suffer smoke" it truly is.

I cover my face with the pillow. I don't want to wake my parents, but the wheezing gets worse. Think about something else ... anything else, but don't think about wheezing.

Sometimes suffer smoke starts slowly—trickling in at the bottom and working its way up to the top. Other times it comes in all at once. It can be just a misty veil so only people like myself know it's there, or so dense you can't see your neighbor's house. Either way, the result is the same. It makes me suffer.

I peer out from under my pillow and look through the screen door at our neighbors' houses perched on the hillside. A full moon bathes their tin roofs in silvery brightness. Suffer smoke wraps itself around the houses like thousands of ghost snakes crawling from the bowels of the earth. Suffer smoke has a life of its own. It knows I'm here and it's writhing its way up to me. It's coming to attack me with its poisonous venom.

The wheezing is worse now. I struggle to breathe. My lungs ache. Frustrated, I start to cry. No, don't—it'll make it worse. Think about something else, anything but breathing. I bury my face in the pillow.

School—tomorrow there's a test in history. I studied hard this evening. My homework is all done. I'll do good on the test. I always do. I've got to get "A's" to go to college. It's the only thing that'll rescue me from suffer smoke. No way I'll get stuck here married to a miner.

My throat closes. I pant—hungry for air. Every second feels like eternity. Air squeezes into my straining lungs. Oh, God, the noise! The wheezing is a roar in my ears. I hope my family doesn't wake up—especially *Mamá*. I crawl into a ball with the pillow on my stomach.

Think about something else. Forget the wheezing. How can I? It's so hard to breathe.

Relax—breathe slower. My *tía* says it works when she has an asthma attack. Hold this one longer. One...two... three—I can't hold it. I have to breathe! I scratch my throat and cry. Now I'm a mess—sobbing, wheezing—not breathing. Please Lord, don't let me die.

Mamá enters my room. "Why didn't you call me?"

She sits on the edge of the bed—pulls my chest down on her lap. Her cupped hand pounds my back. The slow rhythmic movement works on my lungs. I calm down. I stop sobbing— still wheezing but not so bad. How many times has she done this? How many more times before I finally escape the suffer smoke?

"*Ya, ya, está bien,*" my mother croons as she pounds.

A CHRISTMAS STORY

It came to pass, as the year 1921 was drawing to an end, that an economic slump throughout the nation brought woe to the Mexican miners of Morenci. It was not yet the Great Depression, but a difficult time for people used to prosperity. Families were going hungry. A strike by the miners had hardly been settled when the company decided a layoff was in order. The Taylor Dunne Corporation, the one and only ruling power in Morenci, decreed that Mexicans be sent back to Mexico.

The declaration came as a shock—but only to Mexicans. They had lived and worked in Morenci long before T.D. took over the mine and the town. They had abandoned their homes in Mexico many years before. Morenci was now their home—their only home. They set down roots in this new country, built houses, and begot families. How could they be forced to leave?

Anglos were overjoyed. The few jobs left in the mine and the town would now belong to them. The strange people who spoke another language and had such different customs were to be sent away.

The mining company's pronouncement put Javier Aguirre in a double bind. His wife was with child and the family was in debt to Rolando Vegas, who owned the grocery store in their neighborhood. Being a man of honor, Javier knew the bill must be paid before he could leave town. The other worry was how María Isabel, who was due to deliver in a few weeks, would manage on the train T.D. was providing to take Mexicans to the border. Railroad tracks from Morenci descended the mountains in a series of loops like a roller coaster. Javier was afraid the baby might come too soon and not survive.

María Isabel still mourned the infant son who had died five years earlier, poor Leandrito who had lived only to see his first birthday. Javier feared what losing another child might do to his wife.

As the departure date drew nearer, Javier pondered the problem. The solution came to him one night in a dream when an angel of the Lord appeared at the foot of his bed.

"Sell the house to *Don* Rolando and take your family to El Paso."

Not being one to question an angel, not even one in a dream, Javier decided it was the only solution. He went to see *Don* Rolando the next morning. Javier's heart was heavy as he walked up the hill to the little store. Second only to his wife and three children, the house was his pride and joy. It was a gray, two-story home that clung to one of the many hills comprising Morenci. In the yard they had planted a vegetable garden. After the formality of greetings and small talk which were considered good manners among his people, Javier turned to the sad business at hand.

"*Don* Rolando, it is time for us to leave Morenci and I have come to make you a proposition."

"I am sorry to see you go, *amigo*." *Don* Rolando wiped his hands on the dirty white apron wrapped around his corpulent body. He trudged from behind the counter and patted Javier's shoulder. "These are bad times for our people. So many of them being forced to leave. What is your proposition?"

"I would like to sell you my house and everything in it for $300." Javier felt a lump form in his throat as the words tumbled out. "It is a substantial house with a good roof. Two years ago, I painted it inside and out. The garden has many fruit trees."

"Yes, I have seen your house and it is better than the others around it." *Don* Rolando ran a beefy hand through his thick hair.

"If you buy it, I will pay you all I owe. I would have enough money left over to rent a truck and take my family to El Paso." Javier coughed to cover the emotion he felt.

"Why rent a truck, *amigo*? Is not T.D. taking everyone on the train to Palomas?"

"That is so, but my wife is expecting a child and it would not be comfortable for her on the train."

Don Rolando tugged his beard. He closed his eyes as if calculating some figures in his head. "I can offer you $200. I am sorry but that is all. There are others in the same situation and I can afford only so much. It is fortunate you have a good house. Other people have turned their houses over to me just to pay their bills. At least you will have money to rent the truck."

Javier looked into *Don* Rolando's black eyes and read the greed in them. He knew it would do him no good to try bargaining. "It is a deal." He put out his hand and *Don* Rolando pumped it up and down as he walked him to the door.

"Come when you are ready to leave and I will have the money for you. Keep a mattress to make the trip easier for your wife. Consider it my Christmas present!" *Don* Rolando pounded Javier's back.

Javier's spirits sagged as he approached his house. A white picket fence surrounded the orderly yard. He walked through the small orchard admiring the fruit trees he planted as saplings. Each year he pruned them, tending them like a mother did her children. Now they were tall, sturdy, and full of promise for a fruitful harvest—a harvest he would not be here to reap. Tears sprang to his eyes, but he blinked them back. He entered the house and found his wife in the kitchen. He looked at her through his thick steel-rimmed glasses. María Isabel was as tall as he, although stouter in figure compared to his thin and wiry frame. She was twenty years younger, but the age difference was not noticeable. He liked the way she pulled her long black hair into a tight bun.

"Good news! *Don* Rolando has bought our house. I can pay his bill and we have enough money to take us to El Paso. There we can stay with your cousin before we go to Mexico." He hoped she could not tell his cheerfulness was forced.

"You have sold our beautiful house?" María Isabel looked around the kitchen and out the window at her husband's garden. "Why can we not leave it as it is? We can come back when times are better. The last time T.D. laid off the miners, they called them back—remember?"

"Yes, I remember." Javier recalled how he wandered all over the Southwest looking for a job. It was a time of hunger and desperation, but at least then he did not have a family to worry about. He had finally found a job laying track for the railroad in Fresno. It was there he met Artemio Olivario, a man from his hometown in Jalisco. Artemio introduced him to his daughter, María Isabel. The memory of their courtship brought a smile to Javier's face. He spread a calloused hand over her swollen abdomen and gave it a few tender pats.

"This is different, *mi amor*—the company is deporting us. They do not want us here any longer. I must pay *Don* Rolando's bill before we leave and I do not have the money. All we have is this house."

"Then let us sell everything we own and keep the house."

"It is not enough. We need money so we can rent a truck to take us to El Paso. I do not want you to go on the train."

"I can ride it. It will be all right. You will see. Please, Javier, keep the house." María Isabel could not hold back her tears any longer. She buried her face in her apron.

"I cannot go back on my word. *Don* Ronaldo and I shook hands on the deal." Javier hugged his wife as she sobbed in his arms. He felt like crying also, but he was a man—he had to stay strong for the sake of his family.

In the days that followed, Javier and María Isabel put their house in order. They said their goodbyes to friends and neighbors. María Isabel packed their meager clothing and tucked in a few treasures which she could not bear to leave.

She took the picture of *la Virgen de Guadalupe* out of its carved wooden frame and rolled it up to fit in a cardboard box. Javier laid out his tools on the workbench. Years of use had polished the handles of the hammer, saw, and garden tools. They brought back memories of work he had done with them. He hated to leave these precious tools as much as he despaired of leaving his house and garden.

On the day before Christmas, Gustavo Rodela came for the Aguirre family in his one-ton Model T truck. Javier loaded the mattress and quilts in the back and made his wife comfortable. Enrique and Vicente, ages eight and two, clambered up beside their mother, then Gustavo lifted Miriel, four, into the cab. The children were as excited as if they were going on a picnic instead of being banished from their house and country. All three had been born in Morenci and were United States citizens. Javier hoped it would not be difficult for them to adjust to a new country—at least they were used to Mexico's language and culture. He went back to the house for the boxes. The rooms were clean and fully furnished—they appeared as if the family were returning in a few days. Javier took a long last look as if committing it all to memory before he shut the door and locked it.

"Take us to *Don* Ronaldo's first." The old truck lumbered up the hill to the store and squealed to a stop in front of it. Javier prayed it would not break down before they reached Texas. He jumped down and entered the store.

"*Don* Ronaldo, here is the key to my house."

"And here is your money and a receipt for full payment of your debt." *Don* Ronaldo handed Javier $75.

Javier put $50 in a worn leather wallet and stuck it in his back pocket. The rest of the money he tucked into his shirt pocket next to a pouch of tobacco. He pulled out a small piece of paper. "This is where you can send word to us if anything changes with T.D. *Muchas gracias, Don* Ronaldo."

"Your house is safe, do not look so sad. ¡*Vaya con Dios, amigo!*" *Don* Ronaldo waved to them from the door as the truck accelerated down the hill.

Javier handed Gustavo the money from his shirt pocket. "I will give you the other half when we get to El Paso." Gustavo pocketed the money.

As they drove through Morenci, Javier looked around. They had had a fine life here when times were good. God only knew what they faced in Mexico. It had been almost twenty years since he was last there. He dreaded the trip. If times were bad here, it would be even worse there. God help them and all their friends. He shuddered as he recalled people stuffed into railroad cars, their belongings piled high in open boxcars. He had been right to refuse T.D.'s offer.

Fifteen miles outside the town of Lordsburg, after driving through high winds that whipped the truck from side to side, it began to rain. Gustavo pulled off the road and took a canvas tarp from the back. He and Javier managed to lash it over the truck's wooden stakes before the rain sloshed down as if poured from buckets.

Javier peeked in the truck bed before he climbed back into the cab. María Isabel's face was pale and drawn—strands of wet hair plastered against it. The boys did not look happy.

The truck chugged up and down the many dips in the desert road. Javier's stomach did flip-flops and he hoped María Isabel was all right. The rain pelted the windshield so hard, Gustavo could barely see. Miriel whimpered and Javier lifted her on his lap. She vomited just as the truck went through a flooded dip. Water splashed up over the windshield like a tidal wave. The truck went several feet before it sputtered to a stop.

Javier used his handkerchief to clean Miriel's face and clothes. She sobbed and hiccuped. "*Ya, ya*—it's okay, *m'ija.* You're okay." The stench filled the cab.

On the driver's side, Gustavo rustled around underneath the seat. "Here, use these rags to clean the floor." Javier used one to wipe the floor as best he could with Miriel still sitting on his lap. He moved aside the canvas flap on the door and threw the rag out, then soaked the other rag in the rain to clean the remaining mess. He left the flap open a crack, hoping it would clear the smell.

"Looks like we're stuck here for a bit until this rain lets up," Gustavo said. "I cannot check under the hood until it stops pouring."

Javier peered through the rear window at his wife and sons. They lay on the mattress with the quilts pulled up to their necks. Their eyes were squeezed shut as if trying to block out the noise of rain pounding the canvas. He hoped the covering would not leak. Miriel sniffled and he rocked her until she fell asleep. The only sound was rain pelting the roof of the cab. Gustavo never talked unless it was necessary, and Javier did not feel much like talking.

A couple of hours later, the rain tapered off to a sprinkle. Gustavo jumped out of the truck and lifted the hood. He tinkered for a few moments and brought the distributor cap back to the cab. "I think if I get this dry, we can be on our way again."

He dug up some more rags from beneath the seat to dry the part and stretched it out on the dashboard. "By the time it drys, some of those dips in the road will have drained."

Forty-five minutes later, they were on their way again. An hour outside Lordsburg, Gustavo stopped the truck again. "Time for lunch." It was still sprinkling, so the men and Miriel climbed into the truck bed with the others. María Isabel opened a straw bag and distributed bean burritos. The children ate as if starved, even Miriel. Javier noticed María Isabel did not finish her food.

"Are you all right?"

"Yes... it is nothing." She rubbed her back.

"You are sure?"

"I am sure. Let us go. The sooner we get going, the sooner we can be there."

The rest of the trip was uneventful until they reached the outskirts of El Paso. There was a loud bang and the truck swerved. Gustavo brought it under control on the side of the road. "It is only a flat tire."

Javier jumped from the narrow cab to help Gustavo remove the tire from its wooden spoked wheel. When he checked on María Isabel, he saw she was crying. "What is wrong?"

"Nothing!" She closed her eyes and pinched her lips shut.

"Are you in pain?"

"No...it is nothing, I tell you." She waved him away.

"Is the baby coming?"

"No. I cannot have our baby out here in the middle of nowhere. Tell Gustavo to drive on."

"If that is what you want, okay, but I will stay back here with you. Enrique," he called his oldest son, "take Vicente to the cab with Miriel and Gustavo." Javier crouched down beside his wife and held her hand. He prayed they would reach her cousin's house in time.

It was dark when they pulled into El Paso. Gustavo stopped the truck so Javier could come to the front and give directions. They drove until they found the street where Salvador Olivario lived with his family. It was only a couple of blocks from the border separating El Paso from Juárez.

"This is it," Javier said. "Stop in front of that brown building." He looked at the shabby, two-story apartment building. How different it was from his house. At least here they would have a roof over their heads until they could get to Mexico.

Gustavo helped him unload the mattress and suitcases. María Isabel stepped down from the truck bed and clutched her bulging abdomen. "Javier, help me!" A flood of water gushed down her legs.

Javier dropped the mattress and ran to her. "Enrique, go get Salvador." He tried to pick up María Isabel, but she was too heavy. Gustavo came to his aid and the two of them lugged her up the rickety stairs.

Salvador held the door open for them. "Take her to the bedroom." He led the way. His wife, Trinidad, followed them.

"The baby is coming," said Javier. They lowered María Isabel down to the double bed in the tiny room. She stretched out and moaned.

"Salvador, go for the midwife," said Trinidad. "You men wait in the other room." She hustled them out and closed the door.

"Help me bring our things up, Gustavo," Javier said. They went downstairs and carried up the mattress they had abandoned earlier. Miriel and Vicente followed them up the stairs. The men dumped the mattress on the floor and made several trips back to the truck for the boxes.

"Thank you for your help." Javier reached for his wallet and counted out twenty-five dollars onto Gustavo's open palm. "Would you like to stay the night? I'm sure we can make room for you."

"*Muchas gracias.* No—I promised my wife I would get home tonight, no matter how late." Gustavo hopped into his truck and drove off. Javier carted the last heavy box up the stairs. A muffled scream came from the bedroom and he started to go there, but the frightened look on his children's faces brought him to a stop. Salvador's five children were sitting on a bed lined up like birds on a wire, staring at them.

"It is okay. Your *mamá* will be fine. Soon you will have a new brother or a sister." He set down the box and held out his arms. His children ran to him.

The door burst open and Salvador came in with an old woman. She was tiny and hunched over as if the weight of the world rested on her back. Wiry white hair snaked out from beneath a striped *rebozo*. Her face was like a prune—only her eyes appeared young. Javier felt them burning into his when he shook her shriveled hand. Salvador introduced her as the midwife. Another scream, louder than the first, interrupted them and the woman hurried to the bedroom.

Trinidad came out. "Everything is going well. *Doña* Josephina has brought many children into this world. Come, sit. I have made some *tamales* for Christmas Eve."

The children sat at the scarred oak table and Trinidad served them steaming *tamales* from the wood-burning stove in the corner of the room. Salvador and Javier joined them. Javier complimented Trinidad on her *tamales*, but was too worried about his wife to really taste them. They finished eating and the older children helped clear the table and wash the dishes. The younger ones went off to play. The two men sat and talked—Javier keeping an ear open for his wife's cries.

Trinidad went into the bedroom and came back out with nightclothes for her children. "María Isabel wants you." She held the door open for Javier and he rushed past her.

María Isabel lay on the bed covered with a sheet. Tears and sweat mingled on her face. Her hair had come loose from the bun and fanned out like black rays over the pillow. Javier took her hand and kissed it. María Isabel's face contorted in pain as another contraction overcame her.

"It will be a while yet. I just want you to get some rest— put the children to bed." She pushed him away. The midwife signaled to the door with her eyes and Javier left.

In the other room, Trinidad was readying her younger children for bed. Javier studied his surroundings. The room served multiple purposes. Two double beds with tarnished brass bedsteads hugged opposite walls. The stove, table, chairs, a cupboard and a small sink were the only other furniture. He longed for the comfort of his house in Morenci.

Javier retrieved a couple of nightshirts from a straw bag and handed one to Enrique. He undressed Vicente and pulled a nightshirt over his head. Miriel needed help with the buttons on her dress and shoes, but insisted on doing the rest herself. The children crawled onto the mattress on the floor and their father covered them with the quilts.

"*Papi*, is it Christmas yet?" asked Miriel.

"No, not yet. Go to sleep, *m'ija*—tomorrow when you wake up it will be Christmas." He kissed each on the cheek and lay down beside Vicente. *"Buenas noches,* Salvador. *Gracias* for letting us stay with you."

The springs squeaked a complaint as Salvador lowered his bulk on a bed. "What is family for? *Buenas noches,* Javier." Trinidad tucked the last of her children into bed, turned off the light and went into the bedroom.

At first Javier thought he would not sleep with the city noises and the occasional cries of pain from the other room, but he was asleep before he knew it. The angel came to him again.

"You must not go to Mexico. Stay here and find work." The angel's shimmering wings spread out and seemed to fill the room. A golden halo glimmered over flowing white hair. Church bells began to ring.

"Wake up! Wake up! Javier, wake up!" Trinidad shook him. "The baby is coming. María Isabel wants you."

Javier opened his eyes. The bells continued their joyous pealing. It must be Christmas Day! Trinidad was looking down at him. He jumped up and stumbled toward the bedroom. He reached the bed just as the midwife held the baby up. "It is a girl," she said. The baby gulped for air, drew a breath, coughed and cried. "A healthy one!"

María Isabel's head collapsed on the pillow—her face glowing. Javier kissed her forehead and took her hand. The midwife cut the cord and tied it off with a string. She brought the baby to María Isabel. "Your Christmas baby," she said. "Her name is Natividad."

Javier beamed with pride at his wife and the new baby in her arms. The angel had said not to go to Mexico. The new life before him reinforced that message. He could not take his family into the unknown. Salvador would help him find a job here in this country.

So, it came to pass that a child was born unto Javier and María Isabel Aguirre on the one thousandth, nine hundred and twenty-first birthday of Our Lord. A child named for His Nativity—a child that changed the course of history for generations of Aguirres to follow.

The family stayed in El Paso for almost a year until one day Javier received a letter from *Don* Ronaldo. Taylor Dunne was hiring miners again. Javier did not have to think twice—he packed up his family and took them back to Morenci.

Don Ronaldo offered to sell Javier his house back, but he wanted $500 for it. Javier could not afford such a large sum so he settled instead on a dilapidated one-story house nearby. As much as it hurt to see others enjoy his house and garden, and knowing it would never again be his, he was happy nevertheless. As the years passed, Javier remodeled the house and planted a new garden. The births of five daughters after Natividad brought joy to the family.

Each year on Christmas Eve, Javier gathered his nine children around him, sat Natividad on his lap, and told the story of how her birth had saved the Aguirre family from being deported to Mexico. Years later, there were grandchildren and great-grandchildren. By the time there were great-great-grandchildren, the angel had taken Javier to heaven. But no matter—the Aguirre children could picture Javier smiling down at them as their parents told them the story of Natividad.

NO SPANISH ON PLAYGROUND

Mrs. Anderson rang the tiny silver bell on her desk. "Time for recess, children. Put away your work and line up at the door, please."

I did as she said and headed for the door. My best friend, Raquel Mendoza, beat me there and held out her hand for me. I cut in front of someone before I realized it was Duke. He stuck out his tongue as far as it would go and crossed his eyes. Then he pulled up his striped T-shirt, pushed out his white belly, and belched. He looked like a toad.

"Duke Cunningham! How many times do I have to tell you not to do that?" Mrs. Anderson yanked his arm and Duke rolled his pale-blue eyes at me so only the whites showed. "To the back of the line, young man."

Duke stormed away, his spiky blond hair bobbing up and down. I knew he would find a way to get even with me before the day was out. He was the weirdest kid in our first grade class and he made my life miserable. If he wasn't pulling my braids, he was poking me with his pencil. Duke didn't talk much, but he was very physical and always in trouble. It was hard enough speaking English in a class with *gringuitos* for the first time—Duke made it pure hell.

If it hadn't been for Raquel Mendoza, I don't know what I would have done. We were the same size, wore our hair in tight pigtails, and were inseparable. We were each other's life raft in this new world of Dick and Jane. Raquel was my reminder that I had another life and language outside this classroom full of blond, blue-eyed kids who spoke only English. From the start, Mrs. Anderson kept mixing us up, calling me Raquel, and Raquel—Ramona.

I squeezed Raquel's hand as Amanda Smith, holding Mrs. Anderson's hand, led us out to the playground. It seemed that Amanda was always first in line. Maybe it was because she was the tallest kid in the class and probably the smartest, too. She wore a different cotton dress every day in colorful plaids with bright white collars. The dresses were never wrinkled or stained. Her blonde hair, braided with matching ribbons, shined like gold. We all knew she was Mrs. Anderson's pet. None of us liked her much, not even the *gringuitos*—she was too bossy and too perfect.

After Mrs. Anderson gave the word, we scattered to our favorite play areas. Raquel and I rushed to the "house" we had been making in one corner of the playground. It was on a raised patch of dirt near the stairs that led up to the Morenci Plaza. After school, we climbed those stairs to our mothers who waited at the top. It felt closer to home than the rest of the school and was far enough away from the area the playground teacher supervised so we felt comfortable speaking Spanish instead of English. We staked it as our territory and other kids played in it only if we let them.

From our little hill, I looked back at the rest of the playground, searching for Duke. I didn't want to be caught by surprise. The large play area stretched out like a desert in front of Coronado Elementary School. Children were running, hopping, and jumping, glad to be outside after being cooped up all morning. Duke was on the other side of the yard, next to the fence that kept us from spilling onto the road. He was sitting with Amanda under the only tree in the playground.

I turned back to Raquel and our "house." The rooms were just outlines made with large rocks collected from the playground, but to us they were very real. It had taken us several weeks to get enough rocks to build a living room, kitchen, and bedroom. At first other kids had teased us when we scrounged for rocks to add to our collection. But as the house started to take shape, some of them brought us rocks and joined in the building.

Eventually the house was completed and since it was our idea, Raquel and I always determined what we were going to play during recess. Sometimes we decided it was a house and we would choose who would be mommy, daddy, baby, *comadre*, or *nana*. We made up as many roles as there were kids wanting to play. Other times it was a fort and we chose sides for soldiers and Indians. Taylor Dunne Mercantile Store was another favorite, and we would stock the store with things we had seen only in picture books. We shifted the rocks as needed so the house could become one large room or several small ones.

"It's your turn to pick," Raquel said to me. "What do you want to play?" Three girls and four boys joined us, and I decided on something that would send the boys out to the playground so we girls could have the house to ourselves.

"Let's play house," I said. "You boys are the daddies and go fight the war. We're the mommies and we take care of the house. Sometimes you come home on leave and tell us about the war." The boys whooped and raced off to another corner of the playground and we girls settled down to tend the house.

As usually happened in our play, we started out in English and lapsed into Spanish. Some of the *chicanitos* in the other classes didn't speak English as well as Raquel and I did. We had been tested by Miss Griffen, the school principal, a few weeks after school started. After she tested us, she told us to follow her. I was scared silly because she didn't tell us why she was taking us and I was afraid she was going to punish us.

Raquel and I had trailed behind her with our lunch pails banging against our legs. Miss Griffen's dress swished as she limped down the long dark hallway, her high heels tip-tapping unevenly on the tile floor. Her body was hunched—one shoulder lower than the other and her behind stuck out on one side as if a pillow were hidden under her dress. My cousin Tina told me Miss Griffen had had polio when she was a little girl and that's why she was crippled. No one felt sorry for her, though; she was such a mean lady.

I thought maybe we had done something wrong, like we had in kindergarten when we were first learning English. Maybe she was taking us to her office to paddle us, as I knew she had done to other kids. But she stopped in front of Mrs. Anderson's class next to her office. She had moved us from a class with all Chicano kids to one which was mostly *gringuitos*, so now we saw our friends only during recess.

"*¿Comadre*, did you get a *carta* from your *esposo en la guerra?*" I asked Raquel.

"*Sí*. I have a *carta* and it say *que viene en* leave."

"*Mi esposo también me escribió y dice que va a venir,*" Maribel said.

"*¡Qué bueno!* Daddy *viene a visitarnos,*" Ninfa said. She always liked to be the daughter when we played house.

In our role-playing we spoke more Spanish. We were so involved we didn't even notice we had an audience until Mrs. Collins' shadow loomed over us.

"What are you girls doing? You know it's against the rules to speak Spanish on the playground." She wagged a finger at me. "You should know better, Ramona Téllez. And you, too, Raquel Mendoza. Both of you speak English beautifully. You should be setting an example for your friends."

My cheeks burned and I was about to apologize when I saw Duke and Amanda behind Mrs. Collins. Duke was sticking out his tongue and crossing his eyes. Amanda peered at me through her round owl glasses and rubbed her index fingers together, mouthing, "Shame, shame!" I knew Duke had gotten Amanda to turn us in. Mrs. Collins would never have believed Duke.

My anger boiled over and words tumbled out of my mouth before I could stop them. "It's a stupid rule. There's more of us who speak Spanish than there are Gringos. Why can't we talk how we want?"

"*Sí*," said Raquel, "we talk Spanish at home. Why can't we speak it at school?"

"What's bad about speaking two languages? I think it's great!" As soon as the words were out, I knew I had gone too far.

Mrs. Collins' eyes looked as if they were about to pop out of her head. "Come with me, both of you!" She grabbed Raquel and me by the arms and pulled us toward the building. A hush fell over the schoolyard in our wake. I could feel every eye staring as we were led away in shame. The only sound I heard was Duke's loud belch.

Mrs. Collins plunked us down on two wooden chairs outside the principal's office. "Wait here," she commanded, and went in to tell Miss Griffen about our misdeed. I clutched Raquel's hand and whispered in Spanish for her to be brave. Both of us feared Miss Griffen more than anyone else in the whole school. Older Chicano kids claimed she punished *chicanitos* harder than the *gringuitos*.

"We're going to get paddled for sure," Raquel said. Her hand and cheeks were wet with tears. "I've never been spanked before."

"Me neither." I pulled up the hem of my dress and wiped Raquel's face. "Don't cry. She hasn't hit you yet."

"I'm really scared."

"I am, too. Stop crying, Raquel. It's only going to make it worse. We have to be brave." Her tears made me feel like crying, too, but I remembered Duke—so I got angry all over again. "I'm going to pound Duke's fat body into the ground—that toad."

"Duke?"

"*Sí*, Duke. Didn't you see him and Amanda behind Mrs. Cunningham? They told on us."

"*¿Por qué?*"

"Because I cut in front of Duke in line… because they hate us." I shrugged. "You should have seen prissy Amanda's smirk when the teacher grabbed us. I'm going to smash her glasses right into her face."

"I'll help you." Raquel's tears had stopped and she was as angry as I.

Mrs. Collins came out to get us. "Girls—stop that whispering. It better not have been Spanish. You're in enough trouble as it is." She left us in front of Miss Griffen's desk and went out.

"Young ladies, you're in serious trouble." Miss Griffen got up from her chair and hobbled over to us. She leaned her big bottom against the desk. "Look at me when I talk to you." Both Raquel and I were staring at our shoes. Our mothers had taught us it was not polite to look into adults' eyes, especially teachers'.

I put my head up and looked at the painting behind her desk and peeked out of the corner of my eye at Raquel. She was looking straight ahead. Miss Griffen reached out quick as a snake and jerked my chin. "I said look at me!"

I stared into cold blue eyes behind gold-rimmed glasses and gulped. She let go. "As I was saying—you two have broken the rules and now you must be punished." Miss Griffen reached for the wooden paddle on her desk and I flinched.

"This is what happens to little boys and girls who don't behave." She tapped the palm of her hand with the paddle. "But first we need to talk about why we have rules and why we punish when people break the rules." She punctuated each sentence with a slap of the paddle on her palm. I felt Raquel quivering beside me, but I didn't dare look at her.

Miss Griffen continued lecturing us until my legs ached from standing still so long. "You live in America and you have to speak like Americans. We speak English in this school. It's for your own good. That's why we have the rule. I can understand the kindergartners speaking Spanish and some of the kids in the lower first grades, but not you two. You speak perfect English. I put you in the top first grade. There's absolutely no reason for you to speak Spanish."

I opened my mouth to protest, but she glared at me and I snapped it shut. It was just as well. If I had said something, I probably would have spent the rest of first grade in her office.

"The punishment for speaking Spanish on the playground is three whacks, and you get three more for talking back to Mrs. Collins. Raquel, you're first. Ramona, wait outside. Please close the door behind you."

As I shut the door, I saw her yank Raquel to the desk and push her face forward against it. I heard Raquel scream even before I heard the blows. I squeezed my eyes tight and covered my ears, but it didn't help. Raquel's screams and the sound of the paddle on her bottom came through the closed door. My bottom tingled as if I were on the receiving end of that paddle. I knew I would be next, and as I sat there counting the whacks, I swore to be brave—I would not cry, no matter what, when my turn came.

"Look what you've done!" Miss Griffen opened the door and rushed to the sink behind the secretary's desk. She jerked out a handful of paper towels and hobbled back to her office. "Clean it up right now."

I peeked through the door and saw a sobbing Raquel on her hands and knees mopping up a puddle on the floor. "This is disgusting...you're not a baby. Okay, that's good enough. Go down to the nurse's office and see if she has some clean underwear. Come back here when you're dry." She pushed Raquel to the door and called me in.

My heart dropped into my stomach. I looked at Raquel as she squished past in her wet shoes, but she kept her eyes on the floor. I felt her pain and knew it would give me courage. Miss Griffen shoved me to the desk after warning me I better not do what Raquel had done.

The first whack came and I bit my tongue to keep from crying out. It smarted and tears sprung to my eyes, but I didn't let them escape. The second blow was a bit harder and the third even more so, but I was determined not to cry. I had to be brave just like those soldiers who got wounded in the war.

My own father had been wounded and I bet he hadn't cried. I wasn't about to cry just because I was being paddled.

By the fifth whack, Miss Griffen was yelling, "Cry, dammit...cry!" She didn't stop at the sixth one—she just kept on walloping me and wheezing, "Cry!" I knew then I wouldn't cry, no matter how long she kept at it. It was the only power I had over her, so I bit my lip and prayed she would stop soon because my bottom hurt so bad. She must have finally realized I wasn't going to cry because she stopped. I straightened up and rubbed my stinging buttocks. I looked Miss Griffen right in the eyes and held my head up.

She ran her long red fingernails through damp frizzy hair and told me to get out. "Go sit on the chair outside your classroom and stay there until school is over."

At that moment I hated her more than anyone—even more than Duke and Amanda. I knew I would never forget Miss Griffen and what she had done to me and Raquel. I left her office and went to the wooden chairs beside Mrs. Anderson's door. Sitting was too painful so I leaned on the wall. Raquel joined me after a while and we hugged each other. Tears streamed down her cheeks.

"I'm...I'm never going to talk Spanish again," she said.

"Don't be silly. You have to talk to your grandparents and they don't understand English."

"Well, maybe only to them."

"I don't think what Miss Griffen did was right—she hit me more than six times."

"Why? I got hit six...well, actually only five because I peed in my pants before she hit me again." Raquel started to giggle and then both of us were laughing.

"She had to make it up on me for not giving you your six whacks!" We muffled our laughter with our hands. "Ouch! My *nalgas* are killing me."

"Are you going to tell your parents?" Raquel turned a serious face to me.

"Of course! My daddy is going to be so mad, he'll come down here and punch her out."

"He can't do that—they'll put him in jail."

"Oh...yeah, you're right. But I'm still going to tell. What she did was wrong—their stupid rule is wrong." I grabbed Raquel's hand. "I'm not going to stop speaking Spanish on the playground."

"But you'll get punished again."

"Not if my daddy tells Miss Griffen not to, I won't."

"Are you sure you want your father coming down here to talk to her? You know he doesn't speak English that good."

"He speaks it good enough to tell her off." I sounded more confident than I felt. It annoyed me that Raquel had to rub it in. Her dad worked at the T.D. Mercantile and spoke English all the time. My father worked at the mine and didn't really speak much English.

I crossed my arms and plopped down next to Raquel only to jump right back up. It felt as if I had sat on a stove. "Ow! That mean old witch—she kept hitting me just because I wouldn't cry."

We leaned against the wall and watched our classmates file out to the lunchroom. They gawked at us as if we were circus clowns. Duke did his trick with the rolling eyes and stuck his finger in his mouth as if to make himself barf. Amanda did her "shame, shame" again. We ignored them, but I knew I would pay them back someday, somehow. It seemed hours before Mrs. Anderson came back and brought us our lunch pails. "You'll have to eat here. Miss Griffen says it's part of your punishment."

We ate our bean burritos standing up, grateful for once we wouldn't have to listen to anyone teasing us about our food. It was the longest afternoon I ever spent in school. Raquel and I whispered in Spanish and kept an ear open for Miss Griffen's heels tapping unevenly on the floor. She came past us several times and acted as if we weren't there. She didn't even scold me for not sitting on the chair like she told me. Before it was time to go home, I got Raquel to promise she wouldn't ever stop speaking Spanish.

Going up the stairs to my mother that day was a nightmare. My bottom ached so bad, I had to keep stopping. Raquel stayed beside me the whole way. Her sister, who was a senior in high school, had told us there were 357 steps, but that day it felt more like a thousand. When we reached the top, long after the other kids, our mothers ran to us. Raquel started crying again, and I had to tell our story. I could tell how angry our moms were by the spots of red on their cheeks and their pursed lips.

When we got home, my mother took down my panties to check the damage. My bottom was covered with large welts from the paddle. My father was so angry when my mother told him, he wanted to go down to the school right away. By that time, I'd thought it over. Maybe it wasn't such a good idea for him to go. His English was so bad, it embarrassed me.

"No, the principal has probably gone home already," my mother said in Spanish. My parents always spoke Spanish at home even though they knew English. "Wait until tomorrow."

"Then I will go to her house."

"No. It is best to wait."

"Look what she has done to Ramona. Never have we spanked her, and now a stranger does this?" My father slammed his fist on the table. "We send her to school to learn— not to be beaten."

"But Ramona broke the rule and talked back to a teacher."

"The rule? No Spanish on the playground? What kind of rule is that? What do they expect Mexican children to speak?"

Long after I was tucked into bed, I could hear my parents discussing what they would do. The next morning, my father didn't go to work.

"Papa, you don't have to go to school. I'll be okay." I figured if he went, he wouldn't be able to explain his feelings in English and it'd be worse for me when I went back.

"That woman had no right to hit you, and I have to tell her what I think." He was still very angry and I knew nothing I said would change his mind.

He drove me to school in the pickup. I sat on a pillow, but every bump was torture to my sore bottom. We went right to Miss Griffen's office. She smiled and stood to greet him. She looked like a shark zeroing in for the kill. I let go of my father's hand and cowered behind him.

"I here because you beat my daughter."

"Mr. Téllez, please sit..."

"Ramona is cover with bruises," he said in his broken English. "You gave them her, lady. I come say you no hit her again."

I cringed at my father's speech. He was standing in front of her desk with his hat in his hands and I could see him trembling. It was going to turn out just as I had feared. Miss Griffen would laugh at him and take it out on me later.

"Now, please, Mr. Téllez...Ramona was being punished for breaking the rules. I..."

"Six whacks—you no tell her that was punishment? Why you keep hitting her?"

"I can explain...I...I..." Miss Griffen bit her lip and sank into the chair. My eyebrows shot up. This was not going like I thought it would.

"What is rule of no Spanish on playground? Where such stupid rule come from?" my father yelled. "There more Chicano childrens here than Anglos. They come school and speak only language they know—Spanish. It their mother tongue— one that nurture them. Spanish comfort them when they come home crying after day in your school."

"Mr. Téllez...please..." Miss Griffen raised her arm as if to ward off blows.

"You listen, Miss Principal...and listen good. We send our childrens to school learn English, yes—but no for torture when speak only language they know." My father was almost in Miss Griffen's face as he leaned across her desk. I saw her

wipe her face and I swallowed a chuckle. My father had a
large gap in his front teeth and when he got excited, he
sprayed people with saliva.

"We want for our childrens what every parent want. We
want they get good education. I go only eighth grade but for
Ramona and her sisters, I want college. I know she do it. She
work hard in school. Already she talk English better than me.
Ramona speak good English in classroom—so do Raquel.
What it matter you what they speak on playground?"

"But that's the point, Mr. Téllez. They should set a good
example for the other children. How will the others learn English if Ramona and Raquel speak only Spanish to them?" Miss
Griffen was recovering her composure and going on the offen-
sive—but my father would not have it.

"Example? You want childrens no be themselves when
they play? You think they should keep mouths shut because
no speak or understand English? I think girls be better exam-
ples if speak two languages. How you feel, Miss Principal, if
you are little girl in Mexico and teacher no let you speak English—only Spanish and you not know how?"

"But we're in America, Mr. Téllez, and these children all
have to learn English eventually."

"Yes, this I know and they will learn. Do you no think it
better if no shoved down throats? It difficult to learn new language—I know. I learn English most my life and still speak
broken."

I thought at that moment my daddy was speaking the
best English I'd ever heard.

"It scary for our childrens come to your school and learn
English in one year. When Ramona in kindergarten last year,
she come home—cry of headache most every day. She say
tongue hurt from making English words. And many questions
she ask about your customs—most we no can answer." My
father couldn't talk without using his whole body. He pointed
to his head, his tongue, and waved his arms in the air.

"Now you put her with *gringuitos'* class, she come home say they make fun of her food and laugh when she ask things she no understand."

"I'm sorry, Mr. Téllez—I didn't realize...we thought it best to have the children learn English as soon as possible and get used to American customs." Miss Griffen picked up a pencil and scribbled something on a notepad. "I need to think about what you've said and discuss it with our teachers."

"You think all you want, Miss Principal, but I say this—your rule of no Spanish on playground must go. You no get rid of it, I be back and I bring other Mexican parents with me." My father grabbed my hand and stormed out of the room. I kept stealing glances at him in the truck on the way home. I had never heard my father speak so much English before. I sat in awe, not even thinking of my sore bottom.

I didn't go to school for the rest of the week. When I peeked at my backside in the mirror before a bath, I saw a rainbow of colors not found in my box of crayons. I sat on pillows or lay on my belly, the softest chair in the house was too hard for my tender seat. My little sisters benefitted from my recovery time—I started teaching them English.

Upon my return to school the following Monday, I was greeted by Raquel on the playground. "Guess what? Miss Griffen dropped the no-Spanish rule!" I hugged her and we got in line for Mrs. Anderson's classroom behind Amanda. We chattered in Spanish about everything that happened during my absence.

"Duke won't be in school for a while."

"*¿Por qué no?*"

"Miss Collins caught him throwing rocks at cars on the road. Miss Griffen paddled him. We could hear his screams all over the school."

I savored the image of Duke being walloped. But better yet was the knowledge that he was a coward and everyone knew it. "But why isn't he in school?"

"He didn't sit in the chair outside our class. Instead, he came out here and climbed the tree. He fell out of it and broke his arm."

"No need for me to get even with him. It sounds like he got what he deserved," I said, and we both laughed. Amanda turned around and glared at us, but we kept on talking Spanish. No one could keep me from speaking whatever language I chose.

BREAKING THE CHAIN

It was past midnight and Juan knew he was drunk. What did it matter? He had won over a hundred dollars throwing dice. That was more than he earned in the copper mine for two weeks' work.

"*Abre la puerta*, Ana." Juan pounded on the front door of the cottage. "Ana! Where are you? Dammit, open up right now!" He kept calling her name as he beat on the paint-peeled door.

"*Cállate*, Juan. Stop making so much noise." Ana's voice was muffled by the door. "You'll wake up the neighbors. I'm not letting you in until you're sober. I'm fed up with this, *hombre*. I'm sick and tired of being left alone while you go off to gamble with your *amigos*."

She sounded angry so Juan changed his strategy. He fingered the roll of bills in his pocket and decided the money could gain him entrance. He ran a hand through his thick curly black hair and pleaded.

"Ana, *mira*. Open the door, *mi amor*—see all the money I won for you! We can buy anything you want."

"I told you already, Juan, go away—sober up. I'm not going to open this door. I'm going to bed. Good night." Juan heard Ana's voice fade as she walked away from the door.

Juan slumped down in front of the door. "*Vieja*, come back—listen to me. I'm not drunk...only a beer or two— maybe three. Not enough to get drunk. As for gambling—I tell you, I won. Well, maybe I started out losing, but in the end—I won. Ana, answer me. Where are you?"

Realizing that Ana had gone back to bed and knowing her stubbornness, Juan knew he'd have to knock down the door to get in. Not prepared to do that, he decided to go to his sister's house. Shivering in the cold night air, he rolled down the sleeves of his starched white shirt and gave the door a couple of half-hearted kicks. He stuck his hands in his pockets and turned away, feeling dejected. Stumbling out the gate, he found his way down the beaten dirt path leading to the road.

Juan stumbled along the deeply rutted road until he came upon one of the countless footpaths that crisscrossed AC Hill. Sliding easily over the thick water pipe that lay exposed from one end of the town to the other, he surveyed the sleeping town. "¡*Pendejo*! Still stuck in Morenci...still working in the copper mine...still living in a lousy company house...still buying everything from the company store."

When he was discharged from the Army, he'd planned to buy a farm in Duncan. The dream of someday owning his own land had kept him going those agonizing months on the muddy, blood-soaked islands of the Pacific. What big plans he'd made—but he hadn't reckoned with his wife's feelings. Ana had always lived in Morenci and told him she didn't want to move to an adobe house without indoor plumbing. Then there was the matter of *la familia*. Her brothers and sisters all lived in the same town and visited each other and their parents daily. They were not just her family, but her friends and neighbors. She would be lost without them. He knew this was the real reason even though she gave many other excuses.

Juan dreaded going home in the morning. He knew Ana would be waiting to lecture him on his drinking and gambling. He guessed he was unfair to her in that respect, but she was stubborn by refusing to move to the country. Her refusal was why he started going out with his friends in the first place.

"Dammit! I could use this money as a down payment on that land near my brother's farm." The cold air brought him out of his reverie and he staggered on to his sister's house.

Rita's door was unlocked as usual and he went in without knocking. She was sitting at the kitchen table drinking black coffee and smoking a cigarette. His sister's appearance shocked Juan. Only forty, yet deep furrows already marked her brow. Her hair was more salt than pepper, and her plump body sagged in a pink chenille bathrobe.

After their mother had died, Rita had raised him and their three younger brothers. He loved her like a mother. She waited until the youngest was old enough to make his way before she married the only man who courted her. Fernando turned out to be a drunk who beat her. He had abandoned Rita and her girls several years earlier. Rumor was he'd been stabbed to death in L.A., but no one knew if it was true or not. Fernando hadn't returned—no big loss to anyone.

Rita supported her two daughters by selling box lunches to miners and cooking supper for several bachelors. One of these—a tall, gaunt, older man—always had a kind word for her and sometimes brought her girls small gifts. One night after the other boarders left, he stayed. The next day he moved his clothes in and now lived with her. Rita's brothers accepted Pablo because he was good to her, even though the couple wasn't legally married.

"*Hola*, Rita. I've come to visit you." Juan pulled out a chair and lowered himself into it.

Rita looked at him. "I'm glad you've come, Juan. *¿Tienes hambre?* Do you want me to fix you something to eat?" Before he could answer, she ground out her cigarette in an ashtray overflowing with stubs, poured him a cup of coffee, and turned up the flame on the ever-present pot of *frijoles* on the stove.

Juan watched his sister in silence as she busied herself with his meal. Rita deftly turned a flour *tortilla* on the griddle and put it on his plate along with a generous serving of beans. She brought the food to the table and placed it in front of her brother.

The smell of the rich brown beans made Juan realize how hungry he was. He hadn't eaten since lunch because he was in a hurry to gamble after work. Smiling at Rita, he doused the savory *frijoles* with green chili *salsa* and began to eat with gusto.

"How's Pablo?" he asked between mouthfuls.

When Pablo had fallen ill a couple of weeks earlier, they thought it was a cold. Tests showed he had miner's lung disease. It was incurable, and Pablo had grown weaker each day until he was unable to leave his bed.

"He's getting worse. The doctor was here today and wanted to put him in the hospital, but Pablo wouldn't go. Juan, I'm frightened. *No sé qué hacer.* Pablo says he doesn't want to die in the hospital. What's the sense of putting him there if the doctor admits they can't do anything except make him comfortable?"

"You answered your own question, Rita. Let Pablo stay home where he feels secure." Juan felt awkward discussing his sister's problems. They made his sound so minor in comparison. He pushed away the empty plate and lit a Camel.

Rita wiped away tears with a corner of her frayed robe. She reached for one of Juan's cigarettes and he lit it for her. "But I don't want Pablo to die. He's the best thing that's ever happened to me. I don't want to lose him—I've got to do something to save him."

"There's not much you can do, if the doctor can't do it." Juan reached for the coffee pot on the stove and poured more coffee into their cups.

"The other day, Concha was telling me about the old lady who lives next to Madero's store. You know the one—*la curandera.* Concha said her father had once been very sick like Pablo and *la viejita* cured him. Juan, do you think I should go to her?"

"I don't know, Rita. Myself—I don't believe in those things. It's really up to Pablo to decide for himself. Maybe you better talk to him." Juan pushed away from the table. "I hate to eat and run but I haven't been home yet—Ana must be worried." He stood up, ashamed of his lie. It was his duty to stay and comfort his sister, but the atmosphere of impending death made him uncomfortable. Juan hugged Rita and left her alone with her sorrow.

Walking briskly up the hill on the same path he had followed to the weather-beaten shack, Juan was sober. The food and coffee helped, but thinking about his sister did more. He wondered about Rita's life, finding it difficult to understand why she, who always sacrificed herself for others, could be repaid this way. How could God be so cruel?

He stopped and stared at the twinkling stars as if expecting an answer, but the mightiness of the universe made him feel inconsequential. He concentrated on staying on the path until once again he stood in front of the stucco cottage.

Before he knocked, he promised himself he would be a good husband to Ana. He'd stop the drinking and gambling. Getting no response to his knocking, he walked around to the back of the cottage. A sliver of light shone through the bedroom window. Peeking through the parted curtains, he saw his wife sprawled across the bed. A white froth covered her mouth. He looked at the top bunk and saw that his daughter was also foaming.

"*Dios santo*, what's wrong? Ana, wake up!" Juan knocked on the window, but got no reaction. Was she unconscious? He had to get in, but how? He ripped off his shirt, wrapped it around his fist, and smashed the window. Gas fumes assaulted his nostrils. He recoiled in shock. Hoisting himself up on the sill, he reached in to unlock the window. The jagged glass cut his arm, but he didn't notice. Determined to save Ana, he threw open the window and took a big gulp of the cold night air. He put the shirt over his nose and climbed through.

Juan grabbed his unconscious wife and dumped her on the floor before passing out next to her. Minutes later, revived by fresher air at the lower level, he stood up, gripped Ana's legs and dragged her across the floor. He managed to get her into the living room before he was again overcome by gas. When he came to, he realized the only way he could get her out was to crawl and pull her along behind him. It seemed hours had passed before he reached the front door. As he struggled to unlock the door, she began to cough. Not stopping to see how she was, he pushed her out on the porch and ran back into the bedroom.

He yanked his daughter from the top bunk onto the floor. Billy, on the lower bunk, did not seem as affected as his sister. Juan scooped him out of the bunk and left him on the floor. He cradled his daughter to him and crept into the living room without passing out. A hissing noise from the heater made him realize dangerous gas was still leaking. He reached over, shut off the valve on the wall, and continued crawling to the door with his daughter's limp body.

Ana was sitting up, coughing and gagging when he dumped Margie next to her. "I have to get Billy." He turned and crawled back inside. The boy was awake and crying. "I want *Mamá*. I want my shoes and socks."

Juan gathered his son to him and crept through the house. On the porch, he saw Ana holding their daughter on her lap. She wiped away foam from Margie's mouth with the edge of her robe. Margie lay still, her breathing shallow, as her mother tried in vain to revive her.

"She's not waking up. We must get help." Ana looked terrified.

"I'll get my brother's car—we can take her to the hospital. Keep shaking her, for God's sake. I'll be right back." Juan fled down the same path he had followed earlier, grateful that his brother lived close by.

"Miguel, wake up! I need help." Juan opened the unlocked door and ran through the house to his brother's bedroom.

"What is it? Who's there?" Miguel bolted upright and covered his eyes when Juan turned on the light.

"I need your car keys, Miguel. Margie is very sick—I have to take her to the hospital." Juan found Miguel's pants on the floor near the bed and shook the keys out of the pocket. "I'll be back as soon as I can." He ran out the door.

Juan backed the old Chevy out of the ramshackle garage and up the narrow driveway he and his brother had carved out of the hillside a few years ago. Within minutes, he was on the road below his house. Ana saw the car's headlights and ran down the path carrying Margie and half-dragging Billy. Juan got out and helped her lift the children onto the front seat. Ana tumbled in behind them and Juan jumped into the driver's seat and stepped on the gas.

Reaching into the back seat, Ana pulled off the *serape* that covered it. She wrapped it around herself and her daughter. On the floor, she found a towel and used it to wrap around the boy's shoulders.

"I want my shoes and socks, *Mamá*. Let's go home and get them," Billy whimpered.

"Hush, Billy. We'll get them later." Ana patted him on the back and turned her attention to the unconscious girl. "Margie, wake up. *Por favor, Dios*, let her be all right."

The car flew down the road, careening around curves. Ten minutes later they reached the hospital at the top of D Hill. Margie's eyes fluttered open. Color was returning to her cheeks and her breathing was almost normal. Juan opened the car door for his wife and took Margie from her. Ana carried Billy up the ramp through the swinging double doors into the emergency room.

Halfway down the dimly lit corridor, a tall nurse met them and pointed to a treatment room behind them. Her voice was cold and professional. "What's the problem?"

"My family was gassed," Juan replied.

"What do you mean, gassed?" The nurse surveyed the Mexican family and decided they looked healthy.

"The gas heater in our house leaked—it almost killed my family." Juan struggled to control his anger.

"They seem to be fine now. Why don't you take them out for a drive in the fresh air for about an hour? That should perk them right up—no need to wake the doctor." The nurse marched out of the room.

The couple listened to the swish of her starched uniform and the squeak of her rubber soles as she retreated down the hall. Juan looked at Ana. She put her hand on his arm.

"Don't make trouble. Let's do what she says." They gathered up their children and left the hospital.

"Damn Gringa! Who the hell does she think she is? She didn't even bother to check Margie. Dammit!" Juan put Margie in the back seat and slapped the roof of the car. If we were Gringos, you bet she would have fawned all over us. I'm fed up with how we're treated in this town. Chicanos outnumber Gringos and we're still treated like dirt."

Juan's outburst frightened the children. Ana soothed Margie and Billy. She covered them with the *serape* in the back seat and rolled down the car windows.

"Honey, let's do as she said anyway. The fresh air will get the poison out of our systems. Margie looks better already. *Vamonos*." Ana touched Juan's arm and he hugged her.

The couple got in the car and Juan drove away. The houses near the hospital, also owned by the mining company, were larger and in better shape than theirs.

"Look at these houses, Ana. Do you think the company will ever rent us one of those? Never. They save those for Gringos. One of the bosses told me the reason they wouldn't rent these to *Mexicanos* is that they think we're dirty."

"But Juan, they pay more for these houses. We pay only $12 a month for our cottage and they pay $18 or more. We can't afford these houses even if we could rent one."

"They pay more. Sure they pay more because they earn more working at better jobs. When I first started working for Phelps Dodge, I earned $3.19 a day. A Gringo who started at the same time I did got $1.50 more, plus they trained him to drive a locomotive. Hell, if it hadn't been for the union they would still be paying Chicanos less than Gringos."

"You're earning much more now." Ana shivered in her thin robe as the car sped along and the fresh air blew in on them. The children had fallen asleep, snug in the warmth of the *serape*. Juan pulled Ana closer to him and put his arm around her.

"Sure, I'm earning more now. Seven dollars and fifty-two cents a day. Big deal! I work my ass off for that amount while that damn Gringo sits in the cab of a train earning $8.50 per day because he's an 'engineer' and I'm just a common laborer."

They were now driving on the winding dirt roads of *El Espinazo del Diablo*. The houses were built of rough unpainted wood and rusty corrugated tin sheets. As families grew, rooms were patched on to provide more living space. The people who lived in these hovels were the poorest in town. Many of them did not work in the mine or have steady employment. The company didn't enforce a building code and only charged one dollar a year to lease the land under the shacks.

Juan turned off on a road that led back to their own hill. Scattered here and there, in no apparent plan, were larger wood frame houses that looked more substantial than the ones on *El Espinazo*. These homes were well kept and most had fenced-in gardens. They had been built by people who didn't want to live in company houses.

"Why couldn't we buy a house like that with our savings?" Ana pointed to a two-story house.

Juan had been about to tell her he was going to buy a small farm and move the family to the country. He remembered his promise to be a better husband and cringed at the thought of how close he had come to losing them. Instead he asked, "Ana, would you really be happier living in one of those houses?"

"Yes, Juan, I would. My family is here and I don't want to move away from them. Besides, our kids will have a chance for a decent education. I went to high school here and they give you a fair shake if you try. I know you have your heart set on buying a farm in Duncan, but I don't want to raise our children in a community that's even worse than Morenci.

"The schools in Duncan are run by *mormones* and very few Chicano children ever get to high school. The old Mexican schoolhouse is still there. You yourself told me about the outside water spigot that served as your drinking fountain and the dirty outhouse. I don't want our children to grow up in the shadow of that building and what it represents."

"Do you honestly think this town is any better? The best houses are for the Gringos. Look at those nice new houses in Stargo. Those were built just for Gringos. They'll never let a Chicano move into one. I applied when I started working for Taylor Dunne again after the war and look at what they rented us, a death trap. The company had lots of empty houses in Stargo. I drove around there and checked, but when I asked, they told me they were all rented. Do you want to bring up our *niños* in a town where they aren't considered good enough to live next door to a Gringo?"

Ana noticed that they were heading back to the cottage as they talked and she realized that she was afraid to stay there. A shiver ran through her as she thought about what might have happened to her and the children if Juan hadn't come back.

"Juan, let's not argue. I don't want to live with the Gringos in Stargo. All I want is a nice house of our own on AC Hill near my family. We can fix it up the way we want and you could plant that garden you've always wanted." She took a deep breath before she blurted out that she didn't ever want to go back to the cottage. "Let's go to my parents' house," she suggested.

Juan turned off on a side road and parked the car next to a low rock wall. The couple carried their sleeping children down a worn dirt trail. They tiptoed into the house and made their way in the dark to the bedroom Ana and the children had occupied when Juan was overseas. They laid the children down and climbed in beside them on the double bed.

The next morning, Juan woke up early when he heard his father-in-law's coughing in the next room. Turning over, he looked at his sleeping family and wondered what he should do. He got up and was about to leave when Ana's voice stopped him.

"Would you like some breakfast, Juan?" They slipped out of bed, careful not to wake the children, and went into the kitchen. Ana made a pot of fresh coffee, fried a couple of eggs, and warmed a few *tortillas*. Juan wolfed down the food.

"I'm going to take Miguel's car back. I'll stop by the house on my way back and bring our clothes." He pushed his plate back, got up, gave Ana a quick kiss and left.

It was a beautiful morning, a sky so blue it almost hurt Juan's eyes to look at it. He whistled as he walked uphill to the car. Ana was right—an education for their children was very important. He had never gone beyond grammar school but vowed that someday a Sanchez would not only graduate from high school but go to college. If they moved to Duncan, the chances of their children even finishing high school were less. If they had a farm, the children would more than likely be needed to help him work it. By the time he started the car, Juan made a decision.

He drove to his older brother's house, thanked him for the use of the car, and explained what had happened the night before. His brother was expressing his regrets and was about to recount a similar incident in which a Gringo had mistreated him, when Juan interrupted him.

"Miguel, what do you think of that yellow house where the Acuña family lives?" Juan asked.

Miguel gave him a long hard look. "Well, it's a sound house. He rents the downstairs so it brings in a small income. I hear Acuña's asking $2500 for it. Why are you interested?"

"I'm thinking about buying it. Do you suppose we could get them to reduce the price to $2000?"

Miguel lit up a cigarette and puffed on it. "Offer him less than that and he'll jump at $2000. Want to go talk to him?"

"Let's see—with my savings bonds and what I won last night, I can afford to put down $600. I can borrow the rest— my credit's good at the bank. Let's go look at Acuña's house!"

The two-story yellow house stood by itself. It was framed on either side by empty lots full of rubble where houses had once stood. Fires had destroyed both. Juan shuddered when he remembered two children had died in one of those fires.

Señora Acuña opened the door and peered out at them through the screen door. She knew the short, older man was one of her neighbors, but she didn't recognize the younger man.

"We heard that your house is for sale, *señora*, and we'd like to look at it. I'm Miguel Sanchez, your neighbor, and this is my brother, Juan. May we speak to your husband, *por favor*?"

The old lady shuffled away to get her husband, leaving the two men standing outside. Juan examined the house and saw it was well constructed. About five feet away from the house and running its entire length was a rock retaining wall. It was taller than the house. He pointed it out to Miguel.

Señor Acuña came to the door and, recognizing Miguel, invited them to enter. "So you're interested in my house. It's a good house—I built it myself with the help of my sons. Now our youngest son has moved out and the house is too big for just me and my wife. Our oldest son wants us to live with him."

He took the brothers through a short tour of the house. Juan noticed the wooden floor planks below the worn linoleum were in good shape, but the walls needed paint. That was fine with him. Ana could select the colors she wanted. The house was huge compared to his family's three-room cottage. If Acuña agreed to lower the price, he would buy it.

"I like your house very much, *señor*, but where's the bathroom?" Juan asked.

"Ah, of course we have a bathroom. Follow me. It's right out the front door." The old man led the way to a large outbuilding. The brothers followed him up a few stairs and found themselves in a storage room. Mr. Acuña opened a door and proudly pointed out the modern facilities in the next room. "See, we even have a shower."

"*Señor* Acuña, an outside bathroom, even with modern plumbing, doesn't make this house worth what you are asking. My brother doesn't want his family to have to go outside in winter. It's very inconvenient. *Vamonos*, Juan. I hear Fernández has a house for sale with an indoor bathroom and he wants only $2000 for it." They started to leave, but knew they wouldn't get far.

"*Espérense un momentito.* This house is much better built than Fernández's, and you can have it for the same price. The outside of his house needs paint and mine doesn't. Come, I'll show you the downstairs."

They followed the old man past the fruit trees in the garden to the lower part of the house. Mr. Acuña introduced them to *Señora* García and asked her permission to show them around.

"*Señora* García is a widow and she lives here with her two children. She pays eight dollars a month rent."

Juan poked Miguel in the ribs and nodded. Miguel took the hint. "*Señor*, we think you have a fine house here, except for the bathrooms. However, we're willing to overlook that since you've lowered the price. My brother will buy your house."

The three men shook hands on the deal and arranged to meet at the bank on Monday morning. Juan was grateful he had the p.m. shift next week; he wouldn't have to take time off from work. The two brothers left after extracting a promise from the old couple that Juan could bring his wife and children over to see the house that afternoon.

Juan thanked Miguel for helping him. They walked up the hill to the cottage, planning how an upstairs porch room could be converted into an indoor bathroom.

The door to the cottage was still wide open and the gas had dissipated. They entered and Miguel pointed to the ceiling. Juan frowned when he saw how gas had caused the paint to peel off in strips.

"*Gracias a Dios*, I got them out in time or they wouldn't be alive today. Let's check out the heater." They found a rubber hose connecting the heater to the gas pipe had rotted and cracked with age. Juan knew it would be futile to complain to the company, but he yanked off the hose anyway and put it in his pocket. Monday, he would go to the housing office and tell them why he was moving out.

After piling clothes in a couple of boxes, he took a look around the living room, at the humble furnishings and small treasures his family had accumulated. Memories of happy times they'd shared here flooded over him. A peek into the kitchen reminded him of meals prepared and eaten—the first home they'd ever had together. But he wasn't sorry as he closed the cottage door and thought of opening the door to the yellow house. A fresh beginning for his family. Maybe the first step toward breaking the chain.

THE HAUNTED TUNNEL

The two girls finished shopping at Taylor Dunne Mercantile Store and began the arduous climb up one of the many dirt paths leading away from downtown Morenci. Each carried a multicolored straw bag full of groceries. Eight-year-old Natividad trailed behind her older sister Miriel. As she walked, Miriel's long curls swished back and forth. For the umpteenth time Natividad envied those lustrous black curls. Her own straight hair was so fine, it wouldn't stay in braids much less curls. She shifted the bag's handle from one hand to the other. Why had she asked the clerk to pack their bags equally? With each step she took, the bag seemed to get heavier and the sun hotter. Home seemed very far away.

The girls climbed the hills in silence. The strong sun took Natividad's strength; she stopped often to switch the unwieldy bag from one hand to the other. She wished Miriel would slow down. By the time they reached the top of a long flight of stairs, Natividad could not walk another step.

"Wait, Miriel. I have to rest," Natividad called out as she dropped the bag and collapsed on the top stair. She pulled up the hem of her dress and wiped the sweat from her face. Looking up, she saw another set of stairs. They led to the road, and across from it, another set led up to Holy Cross Church. She pictured the stairs in front of the church and the steep hill beyond and her shoulders slumped. The heat was unbearable.

"Miriel, why don't we take a short cut through the tunnel? It's such a hot day and *el túnel* is much cooler." She looked longingly at the dark mouth of the tunnel beyond the stairs and imagined its coolness.

"It may be cool, but it stinks," Miriel said. She set down her bag and leaned on the railing. "Besides, *'apá* told us not to

go in it without one of our brothers. People say it's haunted by
the ghost of Juan Pedro."

"I don't believe that old story. I think it was made up just
to keep us kids out of there. I've never seen the ghost." Natividad stared at her shoes. "I think it would be exciting if we did
see it."

"Have you been going in there?"

Natividad drew circles in the dirt with the toe of her shoe
before she looked at her sister. "Maybe...well, just a few
times...but always with a friend. We hurried through. We
could do that today."

Both girls stared at the inviting tunnel entrance. Heat
rose from the ground in waves. Miriel took an embroidered
handkerchief out of her dress pocket and patted her face dry.
Natividad could see she was beginning to waver.

"It's much shorter than walking up all those stairs. You
can stand the smell for fifteen minutes. Just think of the coolness. If we go through the tunnel, I promise to help you with
your chores tomorrow."

That was all the persuasion Miriel needed. "*Bueno.* We'll
do it, but not a word of this to anyone, understand?" She
picked up her bag and walked toward the tunnel.

Natividad leaped up with her bag and scrambled to catch
up. The girls reached the tunnel's entrance at the same time
and came to a dead stop. Cool air invited them in, but at the
same time fetid odors emanating from the tunnel's depths
repelled them. It smelled like stale beer and damp earth. The
underlying stink of urine stung their eyes. The tunnel seemed
to stretch for miles to a tiny patch of light at the other end.

Once their eyes adjusted, the tunnel wasn't as dark as it
appeared. Every ten feet, a bare light bulb encased in a wire
cage hung from the ceiling, although many were burned out,
leaving stretches of the tunnel dark and spooky.

Natividad knew that if they stood there a moment longer,
Miriel would chicken out, so she plunged ahead. "The smell's

not so bad once you get used to it," she called back over her shoulder.

Miriel hesitated a second before she followed. The girls walked side by side on the hard-packed dirt floor. Beer and coke bottles were strewn throughout. Broken glass shimmered in the dim light like lost jewels. In the corners, where thick railroad posts held up the ceiling beams, piles of paper had accumulated—candy wrappers, newspapers, homework papers, and things Natividad did not care to examine. Most of the clutter was yellowed with age. But the tunnel was at least twenty degrees cooler than it had been outside, and as the girls walked, they appreciated that and ignored the rest.

As always, Natividad was fascinated by the construction of the tunnel. She imagined it looked like the copper mine where her father and older brother worked. Once 'apá had described it to her. Layers and layers of tunnels, much like this one, led off from a central shaft. Sometimes, when Natividad delivered his lunch bucket to the mine's entrance, she peered down the shaft and tried to envision the miles of tunnels catacombing the mountain.

She wished she could go in the mine to see for herself, but she knew this tunnel was the closest she would ever get to it. Women were not allowed in the mine—it would bring the miners bad luck. Natividad wished she could be a boy for a day so she could see the mine. She thought it would be cool like this tunnel, but it wouldn't stink. It would smell of freshly dug dirt. She liked the smell of wet dirt.

When the sisters reached the halfway point in the tunnel, they were startled to hear a sorrowful moaning. Natividad didn't see anyone ahead of them, so she turned to look behind them.

"Where's that coming from?"

"It sounded like it was in front of us at first, but now I'm not sure."

"But there's no one at either end of the tunnel," Natividad pointed out.

"He could be hidden behind one of the posts up ahead," Miriel said.

"Maybe he came in behind us and is hiding back there."

The moaning continued, louder than before. It sounded like a man in terrible pain.

"What should we do?" Natividad whispered.

"Let's run and get help."

The man screamed and the girls bolted in opposite directions. Miriel ran back the way they had come and Natividad ran forward. Miriel glanced back to check if Natividad was behind her and saw her running the other way.

"Nati, stop! You're going the wrong way."

Natividad turned around and saw Miriel at the other end. The two girls ran back toward each other.

"Let's go home," Miriel said. "The man's hurt, he needs help. We can get it faster if we go home."

The girls hurried forward. The moaning continued, and it was definitely coming from in front of them.

"Maybe it's only a drunk," Miriel said.

"Well, if it is, we can hurry past him."

"But what if he tries to grab us?"

"There's two of us and only one of him and he's drunk. We can get away easily." Natividad sounded braver than she felt. The moaning was scaring her and the rectangle of bright sunlight at the end of the tunnel beckoned.

The girls hastened to the exit, hampered by the shopping bags. Natividad looked back at each post as they passed it, expecting to see the man. She was positive that he would jump them at any moment.

Suddenly, the man shrieked and both girls flew toward the exit, abandoning their shopping bags. When they reached the safety of the warm sun, they no longer heard any screaming or moaning.

"He's stopped," Miriel said. They stood at the entrance and stared into the tunnel.

Natividad was prepared to run if the man screamed again. She moved closer to her sister and scrutinized each and every post between them and the overturned bags of groceries.

Miriel nudged her and said, "We've got to get our bags, but let's wait a few more minutes. Maybe he's hiding on the other side of the posts."

The girls stood and peered into the tunnel. After several minutes of silence, Natividad grabbed her sister's hand and plunged in. They ran to the bags and were gathering up the spilled groceries when the moaning started again. It was coming from somewhere between them and the nearest exit—the way they had to pass to get home.

"There was no one there," Miriel said. "I looked behind every post when we came back in."

"Then it's Juan Pedro's ghost!" Natividad yelled. The girls turned and bolted out of the tunnel as if their lives depended on it, screaming the whole way. They were so scared they would have run all the way home, but instead ran into their oldest brother, who was coming down the hill.

"We…we…" Natividad struggled to catch her breath. "We saw the ghost!"

Enrique looked from her to Miriel and saw how frightened both of them were.

"Calm down, *muchachas*. Tell me what happened, Miriel."

"We didn't really see it, but we heard it." Miriel explained what had happened in the tunnel.

"Let's go back to get the groceries," Enrique said. "Don't worry, I'll protect you."

The three returned to the tunnel. At its entrance, the girls stopped and refused to enter. Enrique went in alone and gathered the groceries.

"See, there was nothing there. You probably just heard the wind blowing through *el túnel*," Enrique assured them.

"That was no wind. That was the ghost!" Natividad said.

"We weren't supposed to go in *el túnel* in the first place," Miriel said.

"I didn't know we'd run into Juan Pedro's ghost." Natividad peeked into the tunnel. "Let's make a pact never to go in there again."

"That's the best idea you've had all day, Natividad. If I ever have any kids, I'm going to tell them about the ghost and forbid them to go into the tunnel."

"Me, too," said Natividad. "Let's go home."

That evening at dinner, they told the rest of the family about the moaning man in the tunnel.

"I told you girls not to go in there," said their father. "Juan Pedro was murdered in that tunnel by Salvador Galvan twenty years ago when they were digging it out. They got into an argument and Salvador hit Juan on the head with a pick. Some say it was because they couldn't agree where to place the dynamite, and others think it was because Salvador and Juan were going out with the same woman. Everyone agrees both liked to have a few nips of tequila with their lunch. When he saw what he had done, Salvador left town. No one ever saw him again, but people have sure seen Juan Pedro. Some claim to have seen him with the pick still stuck in his head."

Natividad shivered. "I'm glad we only heard him."

"You were lucky this time. Next time you might not be so lucky. I *do not* want you going through the tunnel ever again."

"Don't worry," said Natividad. "I'm never going near it again."

"Me, neither," said Miriel.

Years passed and Natividad kept her promise. She never used the tunnel short cut again—no matter how hot and tired she was—not even when one of her brothers promised to protect her. Neither did Miriel.

Many more years later, Natividad married, as her sister had done earlier and, even when their husbands were with them, neither could be persuaded to take the short cut. Natividad had three children and Miriel five. When her children were old enough, Natividad told them the story of her misadventure in the tunnel and forbade them to use the short cut. This, of course, made *el túnel* that much more attractive.

One day, Natividad glanced out the window and saw her daughter, Angie and two of Miriel's children standing in front of the tunnel. She ran down the hill, yelling at them to wait. When they saw her, the children stopped.

"How many times have I told you to stay away from this tunnel?" Natividad peered into the dreaded tunnel, remembering Juan Pedro's ghost. The tunnel was darker and dirtier than in her childhood. She shuddered and blocked the entrance with her body.

"It's okay, *Mamá*. We take this short cut all the time," Angie said. "All of us do, and we've never heard the moaning man, much less seen him."

Natividad thought she saw a look of disappointment in her daughter's face. She remembered how much she had wanted to see the ghost when she was Angie's age.

"Go ahead, then. Don't say I didn't warn you!" Natividad smiled as the children went into the tunnel, certain that one of these days, they too would hear Juan Pablo's moaning.

SECRET IN THE SNOW

Something woke Angelina in the middle of the night. She snuggled in the warm bed and tried to go back to sleep. Clink! Pulling the blankets up over her head, she burrowed in deeper. What was she dreaming about? Oh, yes...Bobby. He was asking her to the junior high dance. She should be so lucky. Clink! What was that noise? It came from outside. Her curiosity aroused, she was fully awake now and threw off her covers to peek out the window. An occasional snowflake drifted down from an overcast sky, but there was no one outside.

Clink! Clink! Clunk! The sound was familiar, like digging. Who could be digging at night? Angelina grabbed the quilt from the bed and wrapped it like a *rebozo* around her head and shoulders. She opened the hallway door and heard another clink. It rang out louder. Where was it coming from?

It was not as dark outside as she thought it would be, a full moon shined through the slight overcast, reflecting off the snow. Morenci looked like a postcard in its brilliant, unsoiled whiteness. As she listened again for the sound, snow swirled past the window. The town was silent except for the strange, persistent clinking. Angelina felt as if she were the only person in town not asleep.

The naked branches of her father's orchard trees were silhouetted against the blanket of snow. Snow covered the roofs of the houses that trailed like a staircase down the hill. Their windows were dark and the house next door was dark also. Then a narrow beam of light like a flashlight came from the back stoop. From where she was standing, Angelina could not see all of their back yard, so she moved to the other end of the window. Her breath clouded up the cold window and she wiped it with a corner of the quilt.

In the moonlight Angelina saw a woman in the Mendoza's back yard, digging in the snow with a shovel. Why would the woman be digging in her yard on a night like this? Angelina could see her clearly. The woman wore a short coat that flapped open as she dug. Under the coat, the woman had on a long white dress or—maybe a nightgown? A colorful scarf covered her hair and she wore men's work gloves. Shiny black rubber boots came up to her ankles.

What could the woman be doing? Burying a treasure? Angelina rejected the idea; the Mendozas were not rich. The father abandoned the family long before Angelina's family moved next door. Only the mother with three teen-aged daughters lived in the house.

Angelina's mother did not speak to *Señora* Mendoza and had told her to stay away from the girls. She did not say why, but Angelina guessed it had something to do with the men who visited the house late at night. Sometimes in the summer when the windows were open, she could hear loud music and laughter coming from their house.

One night, Angelina had looked out the window and had seen one of the girls sitting on the back stoop with an older man. They were drinking beer and the man was fondling the girl's breasts. The girl was only a couple of years older than Angelina. She recognized the man. Every Sunday he came to Mass with his wife and five children.

Snow fell and covered the ground as the woman continued digging. The clinks rang out less frequently now. Angelina thought the hole must be very deep. When she was younger, Angelina and her brother had dug a pit in their back yard. After they broke through the top layers of rocky soil, it became much easier to dig.

The woman called out, but Angelina could not hear what she said. A light came on in the kitchen and the back door opened. A daughter, her hair in curlers, dressed in a long robe and fluffy slippers, came out carrying a tiny white bundle straight out in front of her, like an offering. Angelina was reminded of a picture she once saw of the Wise Men carrying their gifts to the Baby Jesus. The girl handed the bundle down to her mother, and as she turned to go back into the house, Angelina glimpsed her tear-streaked face. It was the youngest daughter, the one she had seen on the stoop with the man.

The woman placed the tiny bundle in the hole, crossed herself and leaned on the shovel for a moment, gazing up at the sky as if in prayer. The snow flurried around her as clouds obscured the moon. Angelina barely made out the dark figure as she stooped to shovel dirt into the hole.

An icy shiver ran down Angelina's spine as she realized what the woman had buried. Blinded by tears, the last ones of her childhood, she stumbled back to the bedroom trailing the quilt behind her. She breathed warmth on her frozen fingers and climbed into the cold bed to whisper a prayer.

PLEASE DON'T TAKE THE REFRIGERATOR!

Graciela peeked out the window at the road beyond the yard. Good, the truck was gone. She hurried to a bedroom closet and opened it. "Come on out, kids—the men have left." Her six children filed out of the closet like a gaggle of baby geese. The oldest was fourteen-years old and the youngest, six. Graciela looked at them with pride and wished she didn't have to put them through scenes like this one.

"Why do we hide in the closet when those men come?" asked eight-year-old Fred. He looked up at Graciela with big brown eyes. She hesitated giving him an answer.

"We don't want them to know we're home," answered Tony, the oldest. He was small for his age but mature. Graciela was grateful once again that he was such a responsible kid. Helpful, too—she didn't know what she'd do if he didn't help out with the younger ones.

"Why not?"

"Because we don't want them to take our T.V. and our furniture."

"Why do they want our T.V.?" asked six-year-old Jacob. "Don't they have their own?" He grumbled over to the set and turned it on.

"I don't see why we have to hide," said Karen. She was ten and the only girl in the Foley family. "Why can't we just sit on the couch next time, Mama? I promise to be quiet. That closet is stuffy." Graciela doubted Karen could sit quietly anywhere. She was as rambunctious as her five brothers, if not more.

"Can we go outside now? I want to ride my bike." Junior, thirteen and sullen, was already at the front door.

"I'm hungry," Craig said. At eleven, he was the quiet one in the bunch and tended to get lost in the boisterous family.

"Okay!" Graciela threw up her hands and laughed. "That's enough already! Come to the kitchen and I'll fix you something to eat."

"I bet it's beans, again," Junior whispered to Craig. "They make my belly hurt."

"Beans are okay. I like them," Craig said.

The children followed their mother into the kitchen and the younger ones sat around the large Formica table. Tony set the table while Graciela went to the refrigerator, opened its door, and peered in. Leftover beans from last night's dinner, some tortillas, a few eggs and not much else. Well, they would have to do. She could refry the beans and fry some potatoes her sister Marta had brought over the day before.

Graciela dropped some lard in a cast-iron frying pan and lit the burner with a match. As she prepared lunch, she talked to her children.

"As I've told you before, times are hard because of the strike. When it's settled, your Daddy will go back to work and it'll be better. I've lived through lots of strikes and the men always went back." Graciela finished peeling potatoes and began to slice them.

"When I was a young girl, we used to have fun during strikes because our father would take us to Eagle Creek to pan for gold. That's how we got money to live on."

Graciela remembered another time of need when she was nine-years old. It was during the Depression when the company deported Chicanos to Mexico. It was bad now, but at least things like that didn't happen anymore. She was glad her father had refused to go farther than El Paso. It was the second time her family had gone there—the first time, she hadn't been born yet. Thank God her older sister, Natividad, was born in El Paso. If it hadn't been for her, the Aguirre family might have gone to Mexico and she herself would not be here.

How ironic that Nati and her family had gone to California during this strike.

"Why don't we go panning? That sounds like fun," said Jacob.

"We could use the money to buy something besides beans," said Junior.

"Be glad we have beans," Tony said over his shoulder as he cleaned up potato peelings and threw them in the garbage.

They heard the front door slam shut and all seven of them turned to see who had entered the house. Had the men returned? A shiver of fright ran down Graciela's spine and she felt like telling the children to run. But it was only her husband, Duane.

"I'm home. What's for lunch?" He pecked Graciela's cheek and joined his children at the table. She thought he looked exhausted. There were bags under his blue eyes and his blond hair looked thinner than ever. This strike was taking its toll on him. Every day he went out looking for odd jobs to earn enough money to buy food for them. Some days he came back empty-handed.

"Beans! What else?" Junior scrunched up his nose in distaste.

"Lunch will be ready in a few minutes. Did you find a job this morning?" Graciela asked as she stirred the potatoes in the pan.

"Yeah. I helped Mr. Cisneros muck out his corrals in Shannon Hill. He paid me a dollar an hour." Duane looked through the mail he had picked up. "We got something from Taylor Dunne." He tore open the envelope, read the single sheet of paper and handed it to Graciela—his face downcast.

Graciela took it. "It says here you've been replaced and we have to be out of our house by next week."

"Where will we go?" Karen asked.

"Maybe we'll go to El Paso like Tata did in the Depression," Jacob said.

"Let's go to Missouri," Tony said.

"Does this mean we don't have to go to school anymore?" Craig asked.

"Of course not, silly, we'll always have to go to school." Junior ran his hand over Craig's crew cut.

"Ma—tell him to stop." Craig slapped his brother's hand away. Junior was about to hit him back when his dad grabbed his hand.

"It means we have to find another house—that's what it means." Graciela served the family lunch and sat at the table with them. "I'll call my sisters in Morenci this afternoon and see if they've heard of a house for rent."

"What does 'replaced' mean?" asked Tony.

"I don't know, son. I thought the union was getting close to settling. Something must have happened. I've got to go to the picket line this afternoon—I'll find out what's going on."

The children were excited at the prospect of moving, and argued about where they would like to live. Graciela and Duane ate in silence. She didn't want to think about what "replaced" meant. After lunch, Duane left for the picket line and the children went to the living room to watch television. Graciela was washing the dishes when her older sister Miriel phoned.

"Did you hear the good news?" asked Miriel.

"What good news?"

"The strike is over! The men go back to work Monday."

"The day after tomorrow? That's wonderful!" Graciela said. "Now Natividad's family and our brothers can come home." Miriel said she would call them next.

The sisters talked for several minutes, discussing plans for a family celebration as soon as paychecks started to flow again. After she hung up, Graciela thanked God the strike was over. It had started in July and here it was March, 1960. She thought about the deprivation her family had suffered and shook her head. It was finally over! The letter from T.D. on the table caught her eye. She crumpled it and tossed it into the trash can.

"Kids, the strike is over!" Graciela picked up Jacob and waltzed around the room with him. The other kids danced with each other and kept shouting, "Hurrah!"

Junior kneaded his lower abdomen and said, "No more beans! I'm never going to eat beans again."

Duane didn't come home for dinner that evening and he didn't call. Graciela was worried but didn't let on to the children. She surveyed the larder and found a couple of cans of soup and a can of apple sauce. There was enough cornmeal for cornbread so she mixed up a batter and stuck it in the oven. The children didn't complain about the meager meal. They ate it cheerfully—after all, soon they would be eating all kinds of good food.

That night after the children and Graciela were in bed, Duane came home. Stumbling into the bedroom, he took off his clothes in the dark. Graciela snapped on the lamp. She was shocked by Duane's appearance.

"What...what happened?"

"Our union didn't settle like the others. We're still on strike, but the company has written us off—that's why they sent us that letter saying we're replaced." Duane hung his head then stared at the ceiling. "It's really a company 'lockout'—they don't want us back. They've cut off negotiations."

"How can they do that?"

"Very easy—they own everything."

"But if the other unions settled..."

"We were asking for things specific to our jobs—they didn't want to give them to us."

"Won't the other unions support you?"

"No." Duane sighed and shook his head. "Our leaders met with theirs today and they took it to their membership for a vote. The strike has just lasted too damn long—people are tired of it. They want to go back to work and be able to take care of their families like before."

"So that letter we got today is for real? We have to move out of this house?"

"Yes, and we no longer have any privileges at the hospital or the company store."

Graciela felt as if a dam broke inside of her. All through this strike she had kept her family's spirits up—joking, laughing, thinking up things to do that would take their minds off it. She'd tried so hard to be brave and now when she thought it was over, the worst part was just beginning. Duane held her as she sobbed.

"It'll be okay, Gracie—you'll see. I'll find another job." He patted her back and kissed the top of her head, burying his face in the thick black curls. "You check with your sisters tomorrow and find us a place to live. Let's get some sleep." He pulled her down on the bed and she snuggled up against him.

Duane was soon snoring, but Graciela couldn't sleep. She thought back fifteen years ago to when she married Duane. At first she dated him on the rebound after breaking up with her boyfriend, José, but then she realized she was falling in love with him. It had been a difficult courtship because her parents didn't want her to marry a Gringo. Duane not being a Catholic made matters worse. But Graciela was stubborn and she continued to date Duane. The whole Aguirre family was upset when she announced they were getting married.

At least she wasn't disowned by the family—they had been at the wedding, but she knew they didn't really accept Duane. They still called him "*el gringo*" among themselves. Duane was an engineer on a locomotive—a job that paid more than her brothers and brothers-in-law made. It was also a job they could never hope to get because only Gringos were hired to do it.

Being a Chicana married to a Gringo hadn't been easy. Her neighbors and friends made snide remarks and her family teased her. It hadn't been easy for Duane either. He lost many of his friends and was upset when he couldn't get company housing in Stargo where most Gringos lived. Of course the reason they gave him was that all of the houses were rented. Graciela knew better—she and her sisters had driven through the development and found at least three empty houses. They were finally allotted an apartment in the Mexican section of Morenci.

Even when new houses were built here in Plantsite, the company had kept Gringos and Chicanos apart. Their house was on the lowest level near the tailings with the other Mexican families. The tailings—they were never far from her mind. She was always afraid her children would go off to play there and get poisoned by that muck. The Gringos lived on the levels above—they probably never worried their kids might wander into the tailings.

She hoped Duane would find another job in the Morenci area. No matter how bad things were here, she didn't want to leave. Her family was her anchor. One summer she and Duane went to visit his family in Missouri and were met with less acceptance than they got here. She wouldn't be happy living there.

Graciela tossed and turned, worrying most of the night. The next morning, the family got up, dressed, and went to church. After mass they went to her parents' house.

It was an Aguirre family tradition to spend Sunday together. The whole clan descended on the old couple with food to cook and share. The kids, numbering over fifty, played outside—there were two or three in each age group so no one was ever left out. In the kitchen, the women prepared the food and gossiped about the week's events. The men sat and drank beer on the back porch discussing the same things, but they would never admit it to the women. Clothes the kids had outgrown were brought for younger cousins to wear. Food surpluses were shared—especially in hard times when some family members didn't fend as well as others.

Graciela was grateful she belonged to such a large family, especially now when they were going back to work and Duane wasn't. She knew she could count on the rest of the Aguirres to help her out. Her children wouldn't go hungry.

"Duane has been laid off and T.D. is kicking us out of our house." Graciela had not meant to announce it in the midst of the family's joy over the end of the strike, but the words slipped out before she knew it.

"Oh, that's awful," Laura, her younger sister, said.

"What is Duane going to do?" her mother, María Isabel, asked. She left the stove where she was stirring a *molé* and went to Graciela.

"He's going to look for a job around here. Don't worry, *Mamá*, we won't leave Morenci." Graciela squeezed her mother's shoulders. When had *Mamá* gotten so short? She still thought of her mother as the towering figure of strength she had been when Graciela was growing up.

"I heard there's a vacant house for rent over by the old hospital," Miriel said. "The Cisneros went to California and Fabian got a good job—they don't plan to come back even with the strike over."

"We don't have any money to pay him until Duane gets a job."

"Maybe he'll wait; after all, he's godfather to my Chuey. I'll write to him."

"It would be better if you called—we have to be out by the end of the week."

Just then they heard scuffling noises and yelling out on the porch. The women rushed to the door to see what was happening. Graciela was horrified to see Duane and Laura's husband, Raul, punching each other.

"Stop that! It is no way to act." Graciela's father, Javier, separated the two taller men. "Stop!" A few children who had been playing on the rock patio were now gathered around the porch, staring wide-eyed at the adults.

Duane put his fists down and stormed off the porch. Graciela watched him go up the hill to where their car was parked. "What happened?"

"The men were talking about the strike," *Señor* Aguirre said. "Duane got mad because they told him they voted not to support his union. Raul said some things he should not have and Duane hit him."

Graciela started to go after Duane, but her father stopped her. "Stay, *m'ija*. Feed the children. Give Duane a chance to cool off."

Graciela knew her father was right so she stayed. After the children were fed, the men came into the dining room. She remained in the kitchen and let the other women serve them—she didn't want to see Raul. In the late afternoon, Antonio, Miriel's husband, drove her and the children back to Plantsite, dropping them off in front of the house. Graciela was glad to see their car in the driveway—she was worried that Duane might have gone elsewhere and gotten into trouble.

He was in their bedroom stretched out on the bed, his arms behind his head, glaring at the ceiling. "Your family hates me."

"No, they don't. See, my mother sent you a dish of food. Come into the kitchen and eat. You haven't eaten all day."

He got up and followed her to the kitchen. "I'm sorry, Gracie—I didn't mean to make a scene at your folk's house. It's just that Raul was goading me."

Graciela warmed the food and served him. "Miriel is asking her *compadre*, Fabian, to rent us his house. You'll find a job soon and we'll be okay." She prayed that it would be so.

The next morning, Graciela saw Duane go off to look for work. As she was getting the younger kids ready for school, she heard a knock on the front door. Before she could be stopped, Karen had opened the door. It was the men from the T.D. Mercantile Store.

"I'm sorry, Mrs. Foley, we have our orders." Graciela recognized Pablo Gutiérrez, who was married to one of Miriel's friends. "We've got to take all the things you haven't paid off." He pulled the plug on the television set and carried it out.

The other man consulted a clipboard and took stuff off the sofa. When Pablo came back, they carried the sofa to the waiting truck. Next to go were the bunk beds that Tony and Junior slept in. Graciela and the children watched every move the men made as they carted away the family's belongings. The last item was in the kitchen. Pablo unplugged the refrigerator and the other man started to empty it. At first, Graciela was embarrassed—there was so little in it—but when she saw them load the big Frigidaire on the handcart something snapped inside of her.

"Please don't take the refrigerator! I need it to keep my children's food." She started pounding on the man's arm. Pablo came around and pulled her away.

"Mrs. Foley, please...we're just doing our job." He motioned to the other man to take the refrigerator out as he led Graciela to a kitchen chair. "Sorry," he said, and left.

Graciela collapsed on the chair, put her head on the table, and sobbed as if her heart were breaking. The children stood around her, frightened. They had never seen their mother cry like this before. Tony patted her shoulder and kept saying, "It's okay, it's okay."

Jacob also started to cry, and Tony picked him up to comfort him. Craig and Fred put their arms around their mother. Karen patted her hand. Junior leaned against the door frame and rubbed his stomach as Graciela continued to cry as if she would never stop. The school bus driver tooted the horn twice, but the children stayed with their mother. After a while, Graciela's sobs subsided and she looked up with swollen, red-rimmed eyes. Her children stared at her with concern and love. What was she doing? How could she break down like this in front of them? Tony handed her a dish towel and she wiped her face with it.

"Well, all this means is we have less to pack. Since you kids missed the bus—you get to help me. Come on...let's get started." Graciela jumped up and ran into one of the bedrooms, calling over her shoulder for Junior to bring in some boxes. The rest of the kids hurried after her. They spent the morning packing their clothes.

In the afternoon, Miriel called to tell Graciela that Fabian was willing to wait for the rent. They could move in right away. When Graciela hung up, she noticed a look of pain cross over Junior's face. Suddenly, he threw up. She grabbed a dish towel and clamped it over his mouth while she rushed him to the bathroom. He vomited again as she held his head over the toilet. When he was through, she wet a washcloth and wiped his face and hands. His eyes were glassy. When she felt his forehead, it was burning up. She pulled off his shirt and unbuckled his belt, dumping the clothes on the floor and leading him to Craig's bed.

"My belly hurts!"

"You've probably got the flu. I'll get you some aspirin and you stay here until you feel better." Graciela beckoned the other children to follow her out of the room. "Go pack the clothes in my bedroom. Junior is sick and I don't want you bothering him."

Later that afternoon, Graciela went in to check on Junior again. He moaned and writhed in pain, clutching his stomach. She felt his forehead—it was hotter.

"Mommy, my belly really hurts."

Graciela pulled the covers back and felt his abdomen. It was hard and distended. This didn't look like the flu—maybe it was an appendicitis. Her niece had had her appendix out three years ago and the symptoms had been like this. She had to take him to the hospital right away, but how? Duane had their only car. She remembered her sister Rosa, who also lived in Plantsite, had said her husband was on the graveyard shift. Graciela hurried to the kitchen and called Rosa. Her husband Nicolás answered the phone. He told her he'd be right there.

Graciela called her children into the living room. "Junior is very sick—he needs a doctor." The children looked at her— their eyes wide. "I'm sure he'll be okay, but I want you kids to stay here and wait for your daddy. Tony, you're in charge. The rest of you, mind him. Karen, go find my purse."

When they arrived at the hospital, Nicolás carried Junior into the emergency room. Graciela walked beside them. A nurse behind the counter told them to take a seat.

"No," Graciela said. "This is an emergency—it's his appendix."

"What's his name?" The nurse wrote it down on a form. "Take him in there—I'll buzz the doctor."

Nicolás laid Junior down on the examining table and Junior turned over to one side, bringing his knees up to his chest. Graciela stroked his damp crew cut—she hated to see her child in pain.

Several minutes later, the nurse came, holding a clipboard in one hand. "I'm sorry, Mrs. Foley, but the doctor can't examine or treat your son. Our records show your husband is no longer a T.D. employee. I suggest you get him to Safford right away. If it is his appendix, he's going to need surgery." She bustled out of the room. Graciela and Nicolás looked at each other in disbelief. Safford was almost an hour away. How could they refuse to treat a child? Anger bubbled up in Graciela—she started to go after the nurse but Nicolás pulled her back.

"There's nothing we can do about it." He scooped Junior from the bed. "Let's go to Safford." They were met in the parking lot by Duane.

"What happened?"

"They won't do anything for Junior because you're not a T.D. employee." Tears were streaming down Graciela's cheeks. "We have to take him to Safford."

"No. Put him in the car and wait. Arnold Peterson's son works in the administration office here. I'll go talk to him." Duane rushed toward the main hospital entrance.

Nicolás stretched Junior out on the back seat and Graciela climbed in. She put his head on her lap and Junior closed his eyes. At first Graciela thought he was unconscious, but then he shrieked in pain and drew up his legs. Dear God, please let Duane hurry up—let Junior be okay.

The door to the car flew open and Duane pulled Junior out of her arms. "Dr. Gaines will look at him—Sam convinced him. Thank God, I remembered Arnold was in the union with me." He carried his son off to the emergency room at a trot.

Graciela, followed by Nicolás, ran to catch up with Duane. By the time she entered the hospital, Duane was already in a treatment room and Dr. Gaines was examining Junior.

"It's appendicitis—probably burst. We have to operate right away. I have to scrub—someone will be here to take him to the operating room." The doctor rushed out and a nurse and two aides came in. They flipped Junior onto a gurney. Graciela held his hand as they wheeled him down the hall until they stopped at a pair of swinging doors.

"This is the operating room," the nurse said. "You can't go in. Best wait out on that bench." She pointed down the hallway. "The doctor will come and tell you when it's over."

Graciela went back to where Duane and Nicolás were standing. Her legs felt limp. If Duane hadn't embraced her, she probably would have collapsed. "Junior will be okay now—stop worrying, Gracie."

Nicolás cleared his throat. "I'm going back to Plantsite. I'll pick up your kids and bring them home with me. Rosa will feed them dinner." He patted Graciela's arm. "Don't worry about them—we'll take care of them. I'll call the rest of the family and tell them what's happened."

Graciela hugged him. "Thank you for bringing us," she said.

Duane led Graciela to the bench and they sat down with his arm around her. Graciela felt numb. For the next hour the same prayer kept repeating itself in her mind—dear God, please let Junior be all right.

"Junior was in so much pain—I was scared," Graciela said. "A child needed help and they turned us away."

"Calm down, Gracie. Junior is getting the surgery he needs."

"I'm glad you don't work for them anymore."

"I've been offered another job."

"That's wonderful! Miriel called today and we can move to her *compadre's* house."

"Gracie, the job is in Peru."

"Peru? The country of Peru?"

"Yes—a mining company down there came to our union to recruit engineers."

"But Peru—how can we leave Morenci? My family is here." Graciela shook her head. "We can't go, Duane, please look for another job."

"What if there aren't any? This company is offering more than I was earning at T.D. and they'll pay our moving expenses."

Graciela started to protest again but saw the doctor in surgical greens walking down the hall toward them.

"Mr. and Mrs. Foley, your son came through surgery fine. He's going to have to stay here for a couple of weeks. I think we got that burst appendix cleaned out of there just in time, so there's no danger of peritonitis." Dr. Gaines shook the hand Duane offered him. "You can see him after he wakes from the anesthesia." He walked off to another part of the hospital.

"He's going to be okay, thank God!" Graciela breathed a sigh of relief and buried her face in Duane's chest. "You and the kids are the most important people in my life. I love you all so much!" She looked up at him and Duane kissed her forehead.

"Enough to go to Peru?"

"Yes, enough to go to Peru!" Graciela laughed and pushed him away. "Go ahead and fill out the application and do whatever you need to, but promise me you'll continue to look for something local."

"It's a deal! I don't want to leave any more than you do."

Rosa, Laura, and her mother hurried down the hall toward them. Duane put his arm around Graciela's shoulders and they walked toward the women. Her mother gathered her into her arms and her sisters hugged them both. In the comfort of their warm embrace, Graciela prayed the Foleys would be able to stay in Morenci forever with the rest of the Aguirre family.

YOU DON'T NEED COLLEGE PREP

Antonio was brushing his teeth when he heard Beto's whistle. He spat in the sink, threw open the small bathroom window, and yelled down to his friend to wait. Rubbing a dab of pomade between his hands, he slicked back his black, wavy hair. With a small plastic comb, he carefully shaped a perfect duck tail on the back of his head. He wiped the greasy comb with a piece of toilet paper before jamming it into the back pocket of his low-slung Levis.

In his room, he slipped on a long-sleeved plaid shirt over his white T-shirt, leaving it unbuttoned. A quick glance in the dresser mirror and he flew out the front door to meet Beto at the bottom of the hill.

"What took you so long, *ese*?" Beto cocked his head to look at him.

"I was brushing my teeth."

"You was combing your hair. I know you, man!"

Antonio laughed and slugged Beto's muscular arm. The two boys traversed a steep rocky path to the paved road below.

"Did you pick your classes?" Antonio asked.

"Nah. No need to, *'mano*. The counselor do it for you." Beto picked up a rock and flung it down a ravine.

"The letter said to pick your classes before your appointment."

"That's just for *gringos*, *ese*. Our good old coach, Sherm the Germ, picks our classes."

Antonio stopped and glared at his shorter friend. "Beto, we agreed to get algebra together. What's the matter—you chickening out on me?"

"No, *ese*. I ain't no chicken. You know that." Beto stared at his feet.

"What's bugging you then?"

"It's just that... well... like Old Sherm ain't gonna give it to us."

"How do you know?"

"*Mis hermanos* told me, man. They say old Sherm puts *todos los mexicanos* in voc. ed. No exceptions."

"But there's *mexicanos* in college prep classes."

"*¿Mexicanos o mexicanas?*"

"*Mexicanas*, I guess."

"*Ves, ese*. My brothers don't lie. They been through it already, man."

"Well, I'm still going to sign up for college prep. I need those classes for college."

"You can try, '*mano*. But the counselor, he'll say to you like he say to my brothers, 'You don't need college prep to work in the mine.' Then he'll hand you the list of voc. ed. classes. That's it, *ese*."

"Don't you want to go to college, Beto?"

"That's a pipe dream, man. Sherm the Germ's right. How many *mexicanos* you know in college? If they graduate, they work *en la mina*. If they don't, they still work *en la mina*. We ain't got no chance, man. No chance, no way."

Damn Beto! They had agreed to sign up for college prep classes together—now Beto wasn't even going to try. Antonio was annoyed. Beto was his best friend—they always did everything together. He wondered if Beto's brothers were right. Maybe he should forget about the classes. No! He couldn't give up his dream, even if it meant going in a different direction than Beto.

"I'm still going for college prep."

"*¡Buena suerte, amigo!* I'll say a prayer for you." Beto pretended to give Antonio a mock blessing and Antonio pushed him away. It was a playful gesture, meant to cover up his irritation, but Antonio wished he could shove Beto harder—hard enough to knock some sense into him. Not that it would do any good. Once Beto made up his mind, forget it.

The conversation turned to football, their favorite topic. Before long, the boys reached the high school. Antonio looked at the green, multi-leveled building that stretched across the bottom of the lowest hill in Morenci. This was where he would change the course of his life. He took a deep breath and plunged into its cool darkness with Beto.

They walked down the main hall and saw two of their classmates standing in line in front of the counselor's office. The long hallway was otherwise empty.

"Hi, guys! Sherm's running late," Tillie, who was last in line, told them.

Beto and Tillie chatted about their summer jobs, but Antonio didn't join the conversation. He stared at the dimly lighted corridor. Rows of lockers lined the walls on either side, their reflections mirrored on the waxed floor. He caught a pungent whiff of floor wax, Lysol, and furniture polish. Mingling with the odor were other familiar smells: sharpened pencils, gum erasers, books, and chalk dust.

The school smells reminded him of the new classes he wanted to take this year. Antonio loved to learn and knew an education was his only ticket out of the small mining town. His father and grandfather were miners. Antonio didn't want to follow in their footsteps. They were good men and he admired them, but he felt there was something better in store for him. Thank God his father agreed with him and had been stashing away savings bonds. Every payday, he'd tell the family how many bonds closer they were to having enough money for Antonio's college.

Antonio was glad he also excelled in sports, because his friends respected him and didn't tease him about being a good student. He didn't want to be known as a nerd like those guys who walked around with their pants up to their waists, a slide rule sticking out of their back pockets.

Antonio's thoughts were interrupted by a sharp jab to his ribs. Eduardo, a buddy of his, had burst out of the counselor's office. He looked like a kid who hadn't received the Christmas present he'd asked Santa to bring him.

"Wha'cha get, *ese?*" asked Beto.

"Voc. ed. classes. What else, man." Eduardo waved his class schedule at them as he hurried past, not making eye contact.

"*Ves, ese,*" Beto whispered. "Not a chance. Eduardo wanted algebra, too."

Antonio nodded. Was he fooling himself? What if Sherm didn't let him have those classes. No! He mustn't think like that. He had to have them. Not wanting Beto to further undermine his confidence, Antonio turned to Tillie.

"Are you signing up for college prep classes?" he asked.

She nodded and they discussed the merits of the algebra teacher. Beto pursed his lips and kept silent until Mr. Sherman called Tillie into his office.

"Tillie's smart, *'mano,*" Beto said. "She's been in Gringo classes all through grade school. You watch, *ese.* She'll get college prep."

Antonio was glad a couple of boys lined up behind them, saving him from having to respond to Beto. The conversation turned to football. All four had made the junior varsity team and were excited about playing football in front of a crowd. Morenci townspeople loved the sport and thought nothing of traveling two or more hours to watch a game in one of the surrounding towns.

When Tillie came out, she showed them her schedule. Beto ambled into the counselor's office mouthing "Voc. ed." to Antonio and pointing to himself.

"Did you get college prep classes, Tina?"

"I sure did! But it's a better program than college prep. It's new this year—the Scientific Program. They set it up so you can take math and science courses all four years of high school—supposed to make it easier to get in engineering school. Ask Sherm about it. I've got to run. Bye!"

Antonio was excited. Math was his favorite subject and someday he hoped to be an engineer. The new program sounded ideal, but what if Sherm the Germ didn't let him sign up for it? His stomach churned. He had to convince old Sherm one way or another.

Beto flew out of the counselor's office and yelled, "Voc. ed., man!" The other students in line giggled. As he passed Antonio, he whispered, "I tried, *ese*, but no go. Sherm says my grades are too low. See you outside."

Tears glazed Beto's eyes and Antonio reached out for his arm, but Beto hurried away, his hands stuffed in his pockets. He was whistling, but Antonio knew Beto was covering up his true feelings. He'd seen his friend's disappointment. How would Beto feel if he, Antonio, got college prep classes? Would they still be best friends? Antonio shrugged. He didn't want to think about it.

"Antonio Alvarado. You out there?" Mr. Sherman said. "Come in here. I haven't got all day."

Antonio went in the office and sat on a wooden chair next to the counselor's desk. Mr. Sherman was wearing a white T-shirt with a red wildcat logo and a pair of red shorts. A silver whistle on a chain hung from his neck. Antonio had never seen him dressed in anything else.

"Hi, Mr. Sherman. Thanks for picking me to be on the j.v.'s."

"No need to thank me. You're big and you've got talent. I wouldn't be a very good coach if I hadn't. We're gonna have a great team this year."

"From the way we've been practicing, I bet we beat the Clifton Trojans!" Antonio said.

"Sure we will, but today I've got my counseling hat on— let's talk about your educational program. I've studied your records, young man, and I recommend the Vocational Education Program. We have a very fine voc. ed. program here."

"But, Mr. Sherman..."

"Don't interrupt—let me finish. The next four years, you can take wood and metal shop along with English and math—basic classes, of course. There's general science and your pick of electives, like driver's training. It's rumored T.D. is funding a program in auto mechanics—probably before you graduate—so you'll be able to take it as an elective."

Antonio bit his lower lip. He had to speak up now if he were to get the classes he wanted. But Old Sherm didn't like to be contradicted. It would be so much easier if he kept his mouth shut and didn't rock the boat. The image of his father, dressed in dirty work clothes and a hard hat, popped into his mind. Antonio saw him opening his lunch box, showing him the newest savings bond. The pride in his face so obvious... There was no way Antonio could let his father down. It had to be now.

"Mr. Sherman, I want college prep classes."

"You don't need college prep to work in the mine." Old Sherm was right on cue, just like Beto'd said. Antonio took a deep breath and plunged ahead.

"I don't plan to work in the mine. I'm going to college. I want to be an engineer."

"I'm sorry, Antonio, but you don't have the grades for college prep." Mr. Sherman shook his head and patted the folder on his desk.

"But I'm a straight-A student." Antonio doubted old Sherm had looked at his record, much less studied it, but he couldn't afford to alienate him. He must keep his cool no matter how hard his heart thumped. Antonio stared at the counselor's pink scalp peeking through the blond crew cut.

Mr. Sherman shuffled through Antonio's folder. "Hmm, yes, but I see here you were in low classes throughout grammar school. Those classes weren't challenging like the top ones."

"In junior high, I had classes with students who were in the top classes. Check my grades, Mr. Sherman. I still made A's."

Mr. Sherman riffled the papers and nodded. "Let me check the scores on your last aptitude test. Those are usually pretty good indicators as to college readiness."

He found the test scores and shook his head. "These can't be right."

"Why not?" Antonio's heart stuck in his throat.

"According to this, you scored extremely high. Students don't usually score so high—it's probably a mistake." Mr. Sherman leaned his chair back against the wall.

"Mistake or not, please give me a chance, Mr. Sherman." Antonio was angry, but he knew he wouldn't get anywhere, except maybe expelled, if he showed his feelings. "Let me sign up for the Scientific Program. I can do it. I know I can."

"Whoa there, boy, now you're really getting in over your head. That program is brand new." Mr. Sherman's chair crashed down. "Students will be taking the most difficult classes this high school has ever offered—algebra, geometry, calculus, trigonometry, biology, physics, and chemistry." Sherm counted off the classes on his fingers. "Plus a foreign language, history, government, and college prep English. Sure you can handle all that?"

"I know I can. Please, Mr. Sherman—just give me a chance to show you." Antonio hated to beg, but he was desperate.

"I hate to pop your balloon, Antonio, but it takes money to get into college." Sherman closed Antonio's folder and reached for a class, schedule form.

"I know—I'm working every summer and saving money. My dad's going to help me out also. We got it figured." Antonio held his breath.

Sherman eyed Antonio for a few moments and shook his head like a dog coming out of a river. Antonio was sure he was about to say no. Blood rushed into his head. What else could he say to convince the counselor? His mind was blank.

"Against my better judgment, but...okay. I'll give you a chance. " Mr. Sherman started to fill out the schedule.

Antonio's breath exploded. With a stroke of a pen, old Sherm was about to change his whole life.

"You can find out for yourself. I'm signing you up for college prep classes. If by the end of the year you've got at least a B+ average, you can enroll in the Scientific Program next year." He stopped writing and pointed the pen at Antonio. "Let me caution you...if your grades fall below a C—back to voc. ed."

"Thank you, Mr. Sherman, but don't worry about my grades—I'll do good, you'll see."

Mr. Sherman filled out the rest of Antonio's class schedule and handed it to him. Antonio smiled at the coveted classes listed under his name. But something still bothered him.

"Won't I get behind the other students in the Scientific Program?"

"No *problema*. College prep and the Scientific Program classes are the same in the first year. Don't forget our agreement, Antonio. Any time it gets too hard and you want voc. ed.—come see me." Mr. Sherman waved Antonio out the door.

"College prep!" Antonio grinned at the students waiting in line. He dashed outside and found Beto leaning against the flag pole at the school entrance.

"I got college prep!"

Beto pounded him on the back and reached for his hand. "Put it there, 'mano! Congratulations! No stinking voc. ed. for you, man. You're probably the first Chicano Sherm the Germ's put in college prep."

"Thanks, Beto." Antonio remembered his friend was in the voc. ed. track and his smile faded. He didn't want this to come between them. "Listen, I know you didn't get algebra, but I'll teach it to you. Whatever I learn, I'll share with you. We can..."

SUFFER SMOKE

"It's okay, *ese*...don't worry about it. I didn't really want to learn it anyway. Sherm's probably right. I don't need no stinking college prep to work in the mine. Let's go get a soda, man."

Antonio felt his friend's disappointment, but knew there was nothing else he could do or say to change things, so as they walked back up the hill, he talked about the first game of the season. Football was something they would always have in common.

BLOSSOM IN THE WIND

Angie Benítez eyed Mario Trujillo's muscular arms as he steered the station wagon around another curve on the bumpy dirt road. His bare arms exposed by the tank top reminded her of the label on her mother's box of Arm and Hammer Baking Soda. She wished he would envelop her in those arms the way he usually did. It made her feel secure. Sometimes it seemed there was nothing in the world she wanted more than to have Mario's strong arms protect her for the rest of her life. But was it enough?

If she married Mario, she'd be stuck in Morenci forever—the wife of a miner. Her biggest fear could become a reality. The alternative was to go to college and fulfill her dream of becoming a doctor. For weeks now, she was like a blossom buffeted this way and that by the prevailing wind. What a choice! Her head said college, but her heart insisted on Mario. If only there was a way she could have both college and Mario.

Angie looked at his profile and remembered the first time she ever saw him. It had been in kindergarten. She had been scared after her mother left. The teacher spoke only English and Angie couldn't understand a word she said. Across the table from her was a dark-skinned boy with a head full of coal black curls. He smiled at her and she thought he looked like one of the angels on the bottom of the stained-glass windows at Holy Cross Church. He wasn't afraid of all the strange things they experienced that first year of school. Mario became her guardian angel—her protector against any *gringuitos* who made fun of her mispronounced English.

In fourth grade, the two were separated. Mario's grades had fallen and he was placed in a lower class. Angie lost touch with him until high school. By then, Mario was a heart throb—all the girls were crazy about him, even the Gringas. He had grown tall and handsome. He had a great sense of humor and was very athletic. Angie admired him from afar. He looked like the negative of a picture of Michaelangelo's David. When he asked her to tutor him in English and biology because he needed a passing grade to play football, she was thrilled. That was their junior year. By their senior year, she was wearing his letterman's sweater and class ring.

If only Mario had kept his word about applying to the university, she wouldn't be having to make this decision—they'd be going off to college together in the fall. Angie looked at Mario again. She loved him so much. How could she leave him? she sighed.

Mario had not said a word since they loaded the car in front of the parish house in Morenci. His jaw twitched as if struggling to keep silent.

"Don't sigh like that, Angie. You got your way. We're off to a picnic with a bunch of little boys." Mario kept his voice low and didn't take his eyes off the road. "We were supposed to go on a picnic by ourselves."

In the back of the station wagon, six boys from Angie's catechism class were too busy laughing at silly jokes and punching each other to pay attention to their conversation.

"How many times do I have to say I'm sorry? I promised the boys a picnic if they behaved during classes." Angie wished Mario would at least glance at her. "The boys have been great. I can't go back on my word."

She knew the picnic with the boys wasn't the real issue. It was her indecision about the future—their future. He had been pushing her to make a choice and she wasn't ready. One day she felt as if she couldn't live without Mario, and the next, she knew she had to follow her lifelong dream.

"This is one of our last weekends together before graduation. I planned a special picnic for us—just the two of us. Once I start working at the mine after school is over, who knows when I'll have a free weekend."

The mine. Angie didn't want to hear about work at the mine, but decided against saying anything about it. She was not ready to get into another argument with Mario about their future. "There's still next weekend. We can go then. Meanwhile, can't you lighten up and have fun with the boys?"

"Fun with nine-year-old boys?"

"At least Father Maloney's paying you to drive us to the picnic. I could have found someone else."

"I'm only going because of the money. If I didn't need to buy a pair of safety-toed boots for work, I wouldn't be here."

"Okay—be that way. I don't care. I'm going to enjoy myself even if you don't." Angie crossed her arms and focused on the road ahead. She didn't want to look at Mario or think about the decision she soon had to make.

A trail of dust billowed from a white Ford sedan in front of them. In it were Father Maloney and five other boys from Angie's class. The road leading to Eagle Creek seemed to stretch forever as it went up and down the rolling hills. Angie felt as if she were on a slow-moving roller coaster. She was grateful when the road finally started its descent to the river. It meant they were almost there and she wouldn't have to sit next to Mario any longer.

When they reached Eagle Creek, Father Maloney parked near a grove of cottonwood trees. Mario pulled the brown station wagon up next to the car and the boys piled out of both vehicles, anxious to explore.

"Get back here, boys!" Father Maloney yelled. "Help us unload the food first, then we'll check out the area."

Father wore shorts, a baggy tank top, short anklet socks, and tennis shoes. A baseball cap covered his balding head. Angie was embarrassed to see the priest dressed so informally. She had seen him only in his cassock before, and it surprised her to see his skin was as dark and wrinkled as her brother's old baseball glove. She wondered how he found time to tan in the sun.

"I'm going on a hike up-river. Who wants to come with me?" Father Maloney asked.

"We want to hike down-river," Steve Rojas said. "Larry told us about a bat cave and we all want to see it."

"It's not far from here...maybe three miles," Larry Archuleta said. "Angie and Mario will go with us...won't you...please?"

"It's okay, Father. You go on your hike and I'll go with the boys." Angie was hoping Mario would offer to go, but he kept silent.

"All right. The river's not very deep, so there's no danger. Watch out for rattlesnakes. We'll meet back here at noon for lunch. Mario, are you going?"

"No, Father. I'll stay here and get the fire going for our hot dogs."

"You boys listen to Angie then. She's in charge. See you." Father waved as he walked off.

Angie was disappointed that Mario had chosen not to come with her. She and the boys headed in the opposite direction from Father Maloney. The canyon soon narrowed and they had to take off their shoes and socks. They would have to wade across the river to continue the trail.

"My grandfather used to have a mining claim somewhere around here," Angie told the boys as they were putting their shoes on.

"Copper?" Roberto Martínez asked.

"No, silly. Taylor Dunne owns all the copper," Juan Duarte said. "It must have been gold, huh, Angie?"

"You're right—it was gold. My mom told me she and her sisters used to hike out here from Morenci to help Tata pan for gold."

"He must've got rich!"

"No, they only got enough to buy a few luxuries. It was during the Depression and gold came in handy with ten kids in the family."

"I wish we'd find some gold," Steve said.

They reached another narrow spot and everyone took off their shoes again. They crossed the stream, but it wasn't long before they had to cross again.

"How many more times will we have to do this before we get to the bat cave, Larry?" Angie asked.

"About five or six more."

"Then we might as well keep our shoes on. The path is too rocky to go barefoot."

"My basketball shoes are brand new," Tony Ramírez said. "I don't want to get them wet."

Angie and the other boys plowed through the stream. Tony took off his shoes at each crossing and raced to catch up with the group after he put them back on.

"There's the bat cave!" Larry pointed to a dark gash on a canyon wall. The boys climbed up to the cave and peered in. It was not very deep but it had a high ceiling.

"There must be a million bats sleeping in here. Hurry up, Angie. You've got to see this," Tommy Cervantes yelled.

"There's so many, you can't even see the ceiling," Roberto said. "Let's wake them up. I want to see them fly." He picked up a rock and flung it at the bats. The other boys followed his example.

"Stop that! Leave the poor bats alone. How would you like it if someone woke you up in the middle of the night?" Angie reached the cave's entrance as a few dazed bats circled the boys' heads and bumped into the walls. "The bats need to sleep during the day because they hunt at night."

"Do you think these are vampire bats?" Tommy asked.

"There's no such thing as vampires," Jesus Cueva said.

"Sure there is. My father told me one night at the pit they saw a vampire. It had wings and a cape and fangs!" Tony said.

"If he saw a vampire, then he must've got bit and now *he's* a vampire. Maybe you're a vampire, too," Roberto said.

"Maybe I am and I'm going to suck your blood!" Tony bared his teeth and pretended to go for Roberto's throat.

"Phew, it stinks. Let's go before one of those bats gets caught in our hair." Angie led the way back down to the river. The boys followed, each trying to outdo the other with his imitation of a vampire.

"Hey, Angie, me and my family found Indian pictures carved on some rocks near here. Want to see them?" Tony asked.

"How far are they?"

"Less than a mile up ahead."

"Okay. Lead the way, Tony."

Tony took off his shoes before crossing the creek and the others splashed right into the water. Half an hour and two more crossings later, Tony told the group to stop. He pointed up at a rocky cliff.

"They're up there."

Angie shaded her eyes with her hand. The cliff wall didn't look as steep as the others around the river and there was a trail where other people had climbed before. But it was very high up and Angie's stomach lurched. She knew she couldn't go. Just the thought of looking down from that height made her dizzy.

"You boys go ahead. I'll just sit here and wait for you." Angie cautioned them to climb single file and flopped down on a rock to watch—grateful for a rest. The boys clambered up like monkeys, clutching small shrubs and rocks to help them climb.

Angie thought about the decision she would soon have to make. She wished Mario had applied to the university the way they had planned, but he hadn't even bothered. He decided he'd rather work in the mine. It was too late for wishes— they were graduating in two weeks and Mario was going to work in the mine. Angie hadn't wanted to admit it until now, but if she chose college, they'd probably break up. It would be difficult to have a long-distance relationship.

Angie glanced up and saw Tony grab a bush only to have it come out in his hand. He slid down the steep incline, dislodging rocks as he went. Rocks hailed down on the climbers below him and picked up momentum as they tumbled down, dislodging more rocks. The boys yelped in pain as a torrent of stones bombarded them. Angie watched in horror as a boulder the size of a basketball nearly hit Tommy, the last one in line. Before she could budge, a rock the size of a cantaloupe bounced off Tommy's head and catapulted him backwards. He plummeted down the cliff and landed at the foot of the path.

Angie willed him to get up and tell her he was okay, but Tommy didn't move. She tried to run to him faster, but her legs felt heavy, as if she were trudging through deep mud. Tommy's body lay still, blood gushing from his head. Angie checked his pulse and found it strong. The other boys started climbing down, causing more rocks to shower on Angie and Tommy.

"Stay where you are until I've moved Tommy." She hated to move him, but the others couldn't climb down until they were out of the way.

"Come down one at a time. Roberto, you're the last one so you go first... that way no one else gets hurt."

As she dragged him away from the path, Tommy regained consciousness, moaning in pain. Angie stripped off the blouse over her tank top and used it to staunch the blood. The other boys surrounded them and stared at Tommy. Angie noticed his left leg sticking out at an odd angle.

"Steve, hold the blouse in place on his head. Apply pressure... it'll stop the bleeding. Has anybody got a knife?"

"Here's mine," Larry said.

Angie used it to cut away Tommy's pant leg. She cringed when she saw bone in the wound. "Tommy's leg is broken. Get me some sticks so I can splint it." Jesus and Roberto ran off to get sticks.

"Wha... what happened?" Tommy moaned and struggled to sit up.

"Lie down, Tommy. You got hit on the head by a rock and your leg is broken." Angie pushed him down gently. "I'm going

to immobilize it with sticks. Juan, give me your T-shirt." She
wrapped the T-shirt around the leg and cradled it between the
sticks.

"Give me your shirt, Roberto." Angie tore strips from it
and used them to tie around Tommy's splinted leg.

"Owww! That hurts."

The boys checked each other for injuries, but they had
only minor cuts and scrapes. Angie asked another one of the
boys to take off his T-shirt and she used it to tie her blouse on
Tommy's head wound.

"It's all my fault," Tony said. "I should have been..."

"It wasn't your fault—it was an accident," Angie said.

"Is he going to be okay?"

"Yes, but we have to get him back to the cars. He needs a
doctor."

"Angie, my head hurts." Tommy reached up to touch the
makeshift bandage swathing his head. "I'm so sleepy."

"No. Don't go to sleep, Tommy." Angie remembered reading something about head injuries once. "You've got to stay
awake."

"If two of us make a chair with our hands we can carry
him," Tony said.

"We can take turns, so we don't get tired," Juan said.

"Who's going to be first?"

"Me," said Tony. He slid one arm under Tommy's legs and
the other across his back. Juan's arms gripped his on the
other side and together they lifted Tommy and began the four-
mile hike back to the cars.

"We have to keep him awake, guys, so keep talking to
him," Angie said. "Larry, you and Steve run ahead and warn
Father and Mario that we're coming."

At the first crossing, Tony and Juan plunged into the
stream. Angie noticed that Tony didn't hesitate to get his new
shoes wet. The current pulled at their legs, slowing their pace.
The midday sun beat down on them, draining the boys of
strength and making their hands and arms slippery with

sweat. Tommy's splinted leg stuck straight out, making him even more cumbersome to carry.

Angie and the boys kept asking Tommy questions, but he answered only a few as he drifted in and out of consciousness. They had gone only about a half mile when Juan asked to be relieved. Alberto Cruz took his place and Felipe Ibarra offered to take Tony's, but he refused.

The next time they stopped, Angie noticed that the blouse was soaked and she asked Jesus Cueva to give her his T-shirt. The other boys stood around and talked in subdued tones as she applied pressure to the head wound. She could tell the boys were scared. They'd probably never seen this much blood—she knew she hadn't.

"Let's sing." Angie started singing "Oh, Susannah." After the first few notes, the boys joined in—even Tommy sang. Singing seemed to relieve the tension and it kept Tommy alert.

Angie and each boy took a turn carrying Tommy, but no one could convince Tony to give up his place. He insisted he wasn't tired. Angie thought he was feeling guilty about Tommy's injury.

The trip back seemed to take forever, but as they crossed the river yet again, Mario ran to meet them. Without a word, he took Tommy in his arms and carried him the rest of the way by himself. Angie and the boys plodded behind him, grateful to be relieved of their burden. When they reached the cars, they found Father Maloney had not returned.

"We have to get Tommy to the hospital right away. We can't wait for Father," Angie said. "You boys wait here for him."

"We'll go in the car," Mario said. "Father left the keys in it." He laid Tommy in the car's back seat.

"No, we have to keep him awake. Sit him up." Angie climbed in and Mario propped Tommy up next to her. She put her arms around Tommy and held him upright. He cried out as Mario stretched his legs out on the seat.

"I'm coming, too." Tony jumped into the front seat before anyone could stop him.

On the drive to the hospital, Angie asked Tommy questions, trying to keep him awake and alert. Each time he lost consciousness, Angie shook him gently until he was awake. It seemed as though they'd never get to the hospital.

"Mario, please turn the radio on so we can sing with it."

He did as she asked but didn't join in the singing. His eyes met Angie's in the rearview mirror. She wished he would drive faster.

"If only I hadn't pulled out that bush, Tommy wouldn't have gotten hurt." Tony ran his fingers through his crew cut.

"It's not your fault, Tony. It was an accident," Angie said. "It's nobody's fault. Stop blaming yourself." If it was anybody's fault, she said to herself, it was hers. She shouldn't have let the boys climb up the cliff.

As the car rounded a curve, it spun out and came to a stop facing the opposite direction. Angie managed to hold onto to Tommy so he didn't slide off the seat, but his legs bounced onto the floor and he screamed. Her heart was pounding as she and Mario straightened Tommy's body out on the seat. Thank goodness, she hadn't asked Mario to drive faster. She was about to tell him to slow down, but he didn't give her a chance.

"Don't worry, I'll go slower." Mario turned the car around.

A long tail of dust trailed the car as it traversed the endless hills. When they finally reached the hospital, Mario pulled up to the emergency-room entrance and sent Tony in to get help. Tony sprinted to the door as if his life depended on it. Soon an aide ran out of the hospital pushing a gurney.

"I've got to call his parents." Angie headed for the pay phone and looked up the number. "Mrs. Cervantes, there's been an accident. Tommy was hurt and we've brought him to the hospital. Please come...it's not too bad—a broken leg."

Out of the corner of her eye, she saw Tony sitting on a bench in the hallway, tears flowing down his cheeks. She hung up the phone and went to sit next to him.

"Tommy will be all right. It's not your fault." She hugged Tony and both of them cried. Mario sat next to her and put his arm around her and she turned and sobbed into his chest.

"You did all you could. You probably saved Tommy's life." Mario patted her back. "I'm sorry I was acting so stupid before."

Dr. Gaines came out of the treatment room and they rushed toward him.

"He's going to be all right. He has a bad concussion and a broken leg," Dr. Gaines said. "We've treated the wound on his head and we're taking him into surgery to repair the leg. It should be as good as new when it heals. Whoever splinted the leg did a good job. It kept Tommy from further injury."

"Angie did it," Mario said.

"You did well, young lady. Have you taken a class in first aid?"

"No, I just read a first-aid manual. I treat the injured animals my friends and family bring me, but this is the first time I've had a human patient."

"You might make a fine doctor someday," Dr. Gaines said.

"I'm graduating in a couple of weeks, and I have a scholarship to the U. of A. I want to major in premed."

"Congratulations!" The doctor shook her hand and Angie blushed. Just then Tommy's parents burst into the hospital and Dr. Gaines went to them.

All Angie could think about was what the doctor said to her. She'd never know if she'd make a fine doctor if she married Mario. Angie's thoughts were interrupted by Father Maloney. He came into the hospital and Angie had to report Tommy's condition.

"Angie, you've done a wonderful thing today." Father Maloney cupped her head in his hands and kissed her forehead. Tears sprang to Angie's eyes again, but she held them back.

"You, Tony, and Mario are to be commended." Father shook their hands. "I'm going to stay here with Mr. and Mrs. Cervantes until Tommy comes out of surgery. Would you please drive the rest of the boys home?" He gave Mario the keys to the station wagon and received the car keys in exchange.

When Angie, Mario, and Tony left the hospital, the boys surrounded them—anxious to hear how Tommy was doing. Angie told them and they whistled and clapped their hands, relieved that Tommy was all right.

"Our catechism teacher is a hero," Larry yelled. The other boys cheered.

"Come on, guys, get in the station wagon. We're taking you home." Angie led the way and got in the front seat. The boys piled into the back.

It didn't take long to drive all of them home. Soon Angie and Mario were alone. Mario drove to the lookout over the open pit mine and parked.

"What a day!" Mario turned to face Angie and put his arm around her shoulders.

"Yes, quite a day. In spite of all that's happened today, Marío, I've been thinking about us and I…"

"Wait!" Mario put a finger over her lips. "I love you, Angie. Marry me." He tried to kiss her, but Angie pulled away.

"Please, Mario—I love you, too—you know I do, but…"

"Then tell me you'll marry me."

"I want to, but I also want to be a doctor. I've always wanted to be a doctor." Angie slid over to the passenger side and turned to face Mario. "If I married you, we'd be happy for a time, but then I'd start to wonder what would've happened if I'd gone to college. I don't want to have regrets."

"I'll make you so happy—you won't have any doubts about having made the right choice. You'll make a wonderful wife and…mother."

"Did you hear what Dr. Gaines said to me? He told me I'd make a fine doctor. I'd like to give it a try."

"You're still not sure, Angie. How many other Chicanas have given college a try and not finished? They've come back here and wound up getting married anyway. Why waste time?"

Angie felt as if an icicle had been driven into her heart. Mario had guessed what was really making her decision so difficult. She was frightened of leaving everything she knew in Morenci and going to an unfamiliar situation in college. Although she'd always been an excellent student, she was afraid she'd fail and have to come home in disgrace. Friends who were now in college told her how much harder it was than high school—a couple of them had quit. They said it wasn't the constant studying that got to them—they just couldn't adjust to being the only Chicanas among all those Gringos.

She was scared to go. If she married him, she'd never have to face the unknown. Her life would be like her mother's and her grandmother's—married to a miner, having babies, living in Morenci the rest of her life. That wasn't what she wanted. She wanted to be a doctor more than anything else in the world.

"No, Mario. I can't marry you. It wouldn't be fair. If we got married now, I'd always wonder if I could've been a doctor." Angie took Mario's hand and stroked it. "I love you very much and maybe someday we…"

"Yeah, maybe…someday." Mario bit his lower lip and stared out the windshield. They sat in silence for a long time. Angie's heart raced. She gazed at the open pit mine. The trucks hauling ore on the levels below looked like beetles crawling along an inverted wedding cake. She had made a choice, but she didn't want to lose Mario. She squeezed his hand.

Finally, he spoke again. "I read somewhere if you really love someone, you'll let them go and they'll come back to you."

He breathed deeply and shrugged, still not looking at her. "I love you, Angie...dammit it's hard to say this. I want to marry you, but I..." He turned to face her. "I don't want you to blame me for not achieving your dream. I guess I can wait. Maybe...in a year or two, I can join you at the U of A."

Angie kissed Mario's cheek. She snuggled into his arms.

DELIVER US FROM EVIL

The last notes of "Ave Maria" echoed through Holy Cross Church and seemed to linger in the air. The silence of the congregation was almost palpable, and Tina knew if they hadn't been in church, they would have applauded. She hoped she would be able to sing as well at her high school graduation next month. Tina turned to her friend Lucy with a smile, expecting a congratulatory grin in return. Instead, she was surprised to see tears streaming down Lucy's brown cheeks.

"What's wrong?" Tina whispered.

"Nothing." Lucy wiped away the wetness and managed a weak smile.

"It must be something or you wouldn't be crying. I sang the 'Ave' the best ever and you cry."

"That's it. You sang so beautifully...it made me cry." Lucy took Tina's hand and squeezed it.

Tina looked into Lucy's eyes and knew her younger friend wasn't being truthful. She was about to press the issue, but *Señora* Benavídez, the choir director, shushed her. Something was making Lucy unhappy, and Tina was anxious to find out what, but it would have to wait until after the rosary was over. The priest led the congregation in saying the final Lord's Prayer and both girls joined them. "...but deliver us from evil. Amen." The words echoed in Tina's head. She closed her eyes and repeated the phrase to herself.

Her attention turned to the little girls in white dresses and veils carrying flowers to the statue of *la Virgen de Guadalupe* on the right side of the altar. An altar boy arrayed in a black cassock covered by a snowy white surplice swung a censer back and forth as if he were trying to hypnotize the congregation. The pungent scent of incense mingled with the fragrance of roses, carnations, and fennel. Ferns didn't grow in Morenci, so the Altar Society ladies used the feathery fronds of fennel instead. The smell reminded Tina of when she was one of those little girls. It hadn't been that long ago, but it felt like ages. How innocent she had been. What a thrill to walk up the aisle with the other girls and place the flowers at the feet of *la Virgen*. The only time she felt that way now was when she sang. She squeezed Lucy's small hand and Lucy smiled at her.

"Remember, ladies—tomorrow you must come an hour early." The rosary was over and *Señora* Benavídez was talking. "I want to practice our new songs so we can sing them perfectly during rosary tomorrow. Excellent job on the 'Ave,' Tina!" She excused the choir.

Tina and Lucy followed the other girls down the wooden stairs from the loft. Outside the church, women clustered in several groups to catch up on local gossip. They complimented Tina on her solo and she thanked them as she went past, pulling Lucy behind her. She didn't want to linger and get caught in conversation. Lucy had a problem and Tina was eager to find out what it was. She hated to see Lucy unhappy.

Pluma, Lucy's dog, was waiting for them at the foot of the stairs in front of the church. The tan and white border collie wagged her tail in greeting.

"Hi, Pluma!" Tina bent down to pet her. The collie's tail thumped on the sidewalk.

Lucy squatted next to Pluma and buried her face in the dog's neck. She gave the collie a quick hug and stood up. Tina saw tears misting Lucy's eyes. This was not at all like her Miss Lucy.

"Let's go for a walk," Tina said. She put an arm through her friend's arm and they went up the stairs past the rectory. "Where shall we go? You pick."

"Let's go to the point." Given the choice, Lucy always picked a rocky ledge overlooking the open pit mine.

The girls climbed the hill in silence. Tina thought it best to give Lucy a chance to collect her thoughts. It would make it easier for her to talk about what was bothering her when they got to Lucy's favorite rock.

Tina and Lucy lived next door to each other and, although there was a three-year age difference, they were best friends. Tina remembered the first time she saw Lucy as a newborn baby in her bassinet. She had fallen in love with the infant when Lucy had opened her eyes, looked directly into Tina's, and smiled. Lucy was better than a doll. Tina spent as much time playing with the baby as her mother allowed. She nicknamed her "Miss Lucy Goosey," which she shortened to "Miss Lucy" as Lucy got older.

Lucy's first word, before *mamá* or *papá*, was "Tina." She couldn't pronounce "Justina," which was Tina's full name. Now everybody called her Tina, thanks to Miss Lucy. As Lucy grew up, she followed Tina everywhere. At first she crawled behind her and cried when Tina went home. Later, wherever Tina was, there would be Miss Lucy.

"I'm going to be just like you," Lucy had told her.

Tina always answered, "Of course you are!"

Physically, the two were very different. Tina was tall and slender with fair skin and long black hair. Lucy was short and plump. Her coffee-colored face was topped with a mop of ebony curls that had a life of its own. But, in other ways, the girls were similar. At first, friends and relatives used to tease Lucy for imitating Tina, but eventually they got used to the pair and called them *las cuatitas*, the little twins.

Music was a passion Tina and Lucy shared. Tina had a lovely soprano voice and Lucy's was an alto. Their impromptu duets as they walked up and down the hills of Morenci brought joy to the people who heard them.

Today, however, there was only silence as the two girls climbed *El Espinazo del Diablo* with the dog sometimes trailing behind them and other times running ahead. When they reached the point, Lucy perched on her favorite rock with her knees bent up to her chest. With her white Keds and bobby socks, she looked like a little kid instead of a thirteen-year old. Pluma turned a full circle before jumping up on the huge rock and settling down next to her. Lucy wrapped her arms around the dog's neck and sighed.

Tina went to the edge of the overlook and stared down at the copper mine. The earth was raw and exposed where miners had blasted out the ore. The multi-colored levels of the pit circled around and around, growing progressively smaller until the lowest level appeared as just a dot. Soft shades of pink and turquoise made a striking contrast to the surrounding brown hills, but Tina thought it was too much like looking at a person's insides. Maybe miners perceived the open pit as beautiful. Perhaps they even admired it, the way a surgeon might a patient's organs during an operation, but Tina cringed every time she saw it.

Her father was down there on one of those levels working the p.m. shift. Thank God she'd never have to work in the mine. Come fall, she was off to the university. Once she left Morenci, she was not coming back except to visit her family and Miss Lucy.

Tina looked at what remained of the mountain nearest the pit. Once there had been houses there. Her aunt's family had lived in one of them, but they had to move out when T.D. gave them notice the mine was being expanded. Now the mountain was eaten away and soon would look like the rest of the mine—just a great big hole in the ground.

She sat next to Lucy and put an arm around her. Lucy put her head on her knees and started to sob.

"*Ya, ya.*" Tina patted Lucy's back. "It's okay, Miss Lucy. Tell me what's wrong."

"It's my grades."

"What about your grades?"

"I'm...I'm...I'm failing." A hiccup escaped Lucy's mouth.

"There's no way you could be failing, little one. You always get A's and B's."

"Not this time. I have C's and D's and in algebra I...I got an F." Upon admitting this, Lucy bawled harder. Tina wiped Lucy's cheeks with a tissue.

"It's no big deal. Those grades..."

"But if I keep getting marks like this I won't get into college with you."

"One bad report card won't keep you out of college, silly. As I was going to say, those grades will be averaged with your previous ones and they won't be so bad. You can bring your grades back up in the fall. I'll help you."

"But you won't be here."

"Oh. That's right. I forgot—I'll get Sandy to help you. She's a good tutor."

"Okay," Lucy said. But she didn't look as if things were all right. Her eyes filled with tears again.

"Miss Lucy, I know something else is wrong." Tina held her out at arm's length. "You've always gotten good grades. Why are you failing all of a sudden?"

"Oh, Tina. It's..." Lucy shook her head. "I can't talk about it."

"Why not? We always tell each other everything."

"It's too awful."

"Whatever it is—it's going to keep bothering you until you tell me. Come on, Miss Lucy. It can't be that bad. Tell me."

"It's bad. You're going to hate me."

"No, I won't. Nothing could ever make me hate you, pumpkin." Tina squeezed Lucy's hand and smiled at her.

"Okay, here goes." Lucy took a deep breath. "Promise you won't tell anyone what I tell you."

"I promise."

"I...I don't know how to say it."

"Just say it."

"It's...it's my uncle."

"What about him?"

"He…he's been sneaking into my room at night and… and doing things to me." Lucy coughed and started to cry again. Tina held her close and Lucy clung to her.

"What kind of things?" Tina dreaded hearing the answer, but she knew Lucy needed to unload her burden.

"I don't know how to say it." Lucy gulped and looked up at Tina, her eyes begging for help.

"Does he touch you?"

"Yes, all over in places where he shouldn't. And…and he kisses me on the lips, but not like an uncle. He says he loves me, but what he does is not right."

"How long has he been doing this?"

"Since last Christmas Eve. He came in my room after everyone was asleep and climbed into bed with me. He put his hand over my mouth and stuck his thing into me."

"He forced you to have sex with him?"

Lucy nodded.

"Why didn't you tell me or your parents?"

"He told me not to. He said no one would believe me anyway."

"Oh, Miss Lucy. I'm so sorry this terrible thing happened to you." Tina's anger burnt inside her.

"The next time he came to my room, he said he would kill Pluma if I dared tell anyone. I knew he would do it. You know how he's always shooting at cats. I didn't want him to kill Pluma." Pluma's ears perked up at the mention of her name and Lucy stroked her head.

"We have to put a stop to this," Tina said. "But we have to do it in a way that your parents will believe. We also have to protect Pluma. I have an idea, but first I have to tell you a story I've never told anyone before."

"But you said we told each other everything."

"Yes, but I didn't know how to tell you this when it happened because you were so young. Later, I just didn't want to talk about it. Now I know that was a mistake. I should have told you and maybe it would have helped you with your uncle."

It was two days past my thirteenth birthday and I was excited because we were on the way to spend the weekend at my Aunt Esther's house in Coolidge. I loved to ride in the car, especially on long trips, because then I could read as much as I wanted to and my mother didn't bug me to do something else. *Tía* Esther had moved there the month before and this was our first visit to her new house. She told my mother she had a special present for me, so I was looking forward to getting there.

When we arrived, *Tía* Esther had dinner waiting for us. After dinner, she gave me my gift. I opened the small box and found a single pearl on the end of a gold chain. It was perfect! Before I could ask my aunt to put it on me, her husband Fabián took it from me.

"Here, let me help you." He unclasped it and put it around my neck. As he struggled to clasp it, I felt his rough fingers stroke the nape of my neck. Repulsed, I grabbed the chain away from him and took it to my mother.

My cousin Lily had warned me about him when she lived with us for a few months before her wedding. Lily was *Tía* Esther's daughter by her first marriage. She had told me to keep away from Fabián, but she didn't tell me why. I figured Fabián was probably the reason she had moved in with us. She hated him, and from what little I had seen of him, I didn't care for him either.

While my mother and *Tía* washed the dishes, my father and Fabián sat on the sofa in the living room and talked. My little brother Pedro played with our cousin Salvador. I sat in an armchair and read my book. Fabián drank beer as if it were water and puffed away on an evil-smelling cigar. My dad had a couple of beers, but he's not much of a drinker and refused the tequila Fabián offered him.

As I read, I became aware that Fabián was staring at me. Thank God, I had the book in front of me. Yet, I felt he was looking right through it at my breasts. My father didn't notice because he was too engrossed in conversation. The women came in from the kitchen and joined the men. The others did not seem to notice that all Fabián did was drink and stare at me. It bothered me, but I didn't want to get my parents upset so I just crouched in the chair and tried to hide as much of me as possible under the book.

Finally, my *tía* noticed how drunk Fabián was getting. "Go to bed, *querido*. You're falling asleep on the couch."

Asleep? More like passed out, I thought. Fabián stumbled to his feet and left the room without saying good night to anyone. I felt relieved, but dreaded having to put up with two more days of Fabián.

An hour later, *Tía* showed us where we would sleep. My mom and dad were in the guest bedroom, and Pedro and I were in Salvador's room. Salvador would sleep on the floor in his parents' room. I put on my p.j.'s in the bathroom and, as I brushed my teeth, I remembered Lily's warning. When I went back to Salvador's room, I looked for something I could use to protect myself. I found a baseball bat in his closet and I carried it to bed with me.

My brother dropped off to sleep at once, but I tossed and turned. Even his gentle snore in the twin bed across the room didn't soothe me. I clutched the bat and its hard wood was reassuring. After what seemed like hours, I finally fell asleep.

A hand pulling up my p.j. top awakened me. Another hand clamped over my mouth and I couldn't scream. As I struggled to get free, I tried to say the Lord's Prayer, but the only part I remembered was "deliver us from evil." I kept saying it over and over in my head and suddenly, my hand found the bat. I grabbed it and swung it as hard as I could at my attacker. Thonk! What a satisfying sound! He fell to the floor and I jumped out of bed and kept swinging the bat although I couldn't see much.

"Help! Help!" he screamed. It was Fabián's voice. I hit him again and I heard him throwing up.

"What's going on?" *Tía* Esther turned on the light as she came into the room. "What have you done to Fabián?" She rushed to his side and helped him stand.

Fabián was bleeding from a couple of places on his head. Good, I thought. I wished I'd connected with the bat many more times. My parents ran in and everyone began yelling at each other. Pedro sat on his bed and whimpered.

"What was Fabián doing in Tina's room?" my father asked.

"Look what your daughter did to Fabián's head. He's bleeding to death." Fabián moaned as if he were dying and clutched something at his stomach.

"Tina wouldn't have hit him without a reason. What was he doing in here?" my mother asked. She put a protective arm around me.

"This is Salvador's room. He forgot Tina and Pedro were in here tonight and probably came to check on Salvador. Usually he does that at night."

"No," I said. "He wasn't checking on Salvador. He pulled up my pajama top and felt me."

"You're crazy. Fabián would never do a thing like that. You're his niece."

"Wake up, Esther. You know what Fabián is capable of. Why do you think Lily moved out of your house? I'll teach him to molest young girls." My father grabbed Fabián's shirt and was about to pop him one when my aunt got between them. Fabián stumbled back against the wall and his pants fell around his ankles. He jerked them back up and fumbled with the buttons.

"I'm going to kill him." My father advanced on Fabián again, but my mother tugged him away.

"No. Let's get out of here. Tina's not hurt, *gracias a Dios*, and it looks like Fabián got the worst of it."

"Yes, please leave. Fabián was drunk. He didn't know what he was doing." My aunt shoved her husband out of the room and down the hall to their room.

Salvador stood in the hallway rubbing his eyes. "What's happening?" When no one answered, he padded into the bathroom and closed the door.

My father shook free of my mother and tried to open *Tía's* door, but it was locked. He pounded on it with his fist. "Don't you dare show your face in Morenci again, Fabián. What Tina did to you with that bat is nothing compared to what I'll do to you."

"Gather your things, kids. We're going home." My mother pulled my father into the guest bedroom. I looked at Pedro and started shaking. When my parents came back fully dressed, they found me still in my p.j.'s with tears streaming down my face. Pedro sat next to me on the bed, patting my hand.

"It's okay. Tina. It's all over. You're safe now." My mother hugged me and slipped a sweater over my pajamas.

"Let's go," my father said. His jaw was twitching as he carried our suitcase to the car.

Even with the sweater on, I couldn't stop trembling. My tears flowed.

"Sit up here in front," my mother said. "The heater will warm you up a lot faster."

I sat in the front between my parents and we drove home without a word. The only sound in the car was my teeth chattering. The clock in the dashboard marked 4:30. It was dark when we left my *tía's* house, but as my father steered the car on the empty highway, the rising sun greeted us.

"My parents never discussed what happened to me, so I felt it was something they wanted to keep hidden. My cousin Lily, the only person I could talk to, had moved to California and I never told anyone until now." Tina was shivering when she finished her story. Tears streamed down her cheeks and she wiped them away with her fingers.

"You were so brave." Lucy hugged Tina's arm. "I wish I could've done what you did. If I had, my uncle would've stopped bothering me long ago."

"Don't blame yourself, *m'ija*. It's not your fault. No one warned you about him. How could you know? What we have to do now is come up with a plan so he's stopped."

"What can we do? The only way my parents will believe me is if he's caught in the act."

"That's it. We're going to make sure he gets caught. You take your brother's bat to bed with you every night and be prepared to use it."

"No problem. I could hit him with it right now. I'd whack him so hard his head would fall off. I hate his guts."

"Calm down, Miss Lucy. You have to act the same as always. We don't want him to get suspicious. Next time he gets in your bed, clobber him with all your strength and scream your head off. That'll bring your parents to your room and they'll see what a nasty man he is."

"Can I hit him again?"

"You can hit him as many times as you like." Tina laughed and ruffled Lucy's curls.

"Then I'll hit him again and again. I'll hit him as many times as he hurt me. He's going to be so bloody—they'll have to take him to the hospital. Maybe I'll give him a concussion." Lucy was the happiest Tina had seen her in a long time.

"Be sure to wait until he has his pants down so your parents will have no doubt about what he was up to."

"Thanks, Tina, you always come through for me. I should have told you about this earlier. I'm going to clobber him so hard, he's going to wish he'd never messed with me." Lucy whacked her fist against the palm of her other hand.

"Just don't kill him. We don't want you landing in jail."

"He's the one who should be put in jail for what he did to me."

"Don't get your hopes up. Remember, he's your mother's brother and you know how she is about family. She probably won't want to turn him in, but at least she'll make sure he stays away from you. Hey, it's getting dark." Tina pulled Lucy up off the rock. "Time to go home, Miss Lucy."

Several days later, Tina was studying in her bedroom when Lucy ran in—grinning from ear to ear. "Armando's gone!" She flung herself on the bed next to Tina.

"Tell me what happened." Tina dropped her book. Both girls sat up Indian-style, facing each other.

"I did just what you said. When my parents saw him, all bloody with his pants down to his ankles, my father took the bat from me. *Mamá* had to take it away from him before he used it on Armando."

"Too bad!"

"It was okay. It didn't stop *Papá* from beating him up. Armando crawled to his room and locked the door. My mother yelled at him to pack his things and be gone by morning." Lucy laughed and clapped her hands. "This morning he was gone! No more Armando!"

"Did you tell your parents what he had been doing?"

A serious look came over Lucy's face. "After all the excitement was over, I lost it. I couldn't stop crying till I threw up. While *Mamá* was cleaning up—I told her. She cried and hugged me so tight, I thought I'd suffocate. Then she got mad—I've never seen her that angry. She pounded on Armando's door until my father stopped her. Then she came in my room, shut the door behind her, and told me not to tell anyone what happened—not even *Papá*. It made me feel as if I had done something wrong, too."

"Don't even think it. You didn't do anything wrong, peanut—it was all Armando's doing." Tina pinched her lips together before continuing. "Remember I told you my parents didn't want to talk about it either after I was attacked? It seemed as if keeping silent let them pretend it never happened. Not talking about it made it worse for me. I kept having the same nightmare—a really scary one."

Tina squeezed her eyes shut and shook her head back and forth as if to block out images only she saw. Lucy clasped her hand, prompting Tina to go on.

"In the nightmare, I'd feel a heavy weight on top of me and I'd wake up to see a man holding a butcher knife. I'd be frozen—not able to move or scream. Just as he was plunging the knife into me, I'd wake up in a cold sweat." Tina turned to look into Lucy's eyes.

"Since I told you about it, I haven't had any more nightmares. I think telling you helped me. Maybe when you need to talk about what your uncle did to you, you should tell me. Don't keep your feelings locked up like I did."

"It's a deal!" Lucy shook Tina's hand—a grin on her face. "And you promise to talk to me when you need to."

"Don't worry, I will." Tina smiled at her friend's exuberance as Lucy pumped her hand up and down. "Let's go for a walk, Miss Lucy." She jumped off the bed, pulling Lucy behind her.

Pluma was waiting for them outside on the patio. She wagged her tail and followed the girls to the gate. Before opening it, Tina picked up Lucy in a bear hug and swung her around like she used to when Lucy was younger. Lucy giggled and Pluma barked at them. The mulberry tree, potted red geraniums, rose bushes, and blue sky above went around and around until everything was a blur of color like in a kaleidoscope. Tina was laughing so hard she had to set Lucy down. Both of them collapsed on the patio floor in a jumble of arms and legs. Pluma licked their faces and the girls laughed.

THE HITCHHIKING MARIACHI

Alberto Martínez yawned and shook his head vigorously. Dammit! He should have slept longer today. He hated the graveyard shift at the mine. The drive to work was the hard part. The long straight stretch from Safford to the mountains made him drowsy, but once he hit the road that snaked through the foothills, he became alert. Maneuvering the truck around the curves occupied his full attention.

At the last curve before the road dropped to the Gila River Bridge, Alberto saw a young man waving a large Mexican *sombrero*. Alberto drove past him before he thought to stop. The man ran up to the truck and opened the passenger door.

"*Gracias, 'mano.* I need to get to Clifton."

"Sure. Hop in. I'm on my way to the pit."

In the instant before the door slammed shut, Alberto caught a glimpse of the hitchhiker. He was wearing a short black mariachi jacket and tight pants studded with silver conchos. A starched white shirt and red fluffy bow tie completed the outfit.

"My name is Alberto." He reached over and shook the man's hand. It felt cold. Strange. It was at least 90 degrees outside.

"I'm David Orozco."

"Kind of late to be hitching a ride out here in the middle of nowhere."

"I was on my way back to Clifton and I had a little car trouble."

"Car trouble? I didn't see your car."

"I missed that curve back there and my car went off the road."

"Are you all right?" Alberto looked over at David. In the dim light of the instrument panel, he saw the youth was unscathed. Not a hair out of place and the shirt wasn't even wrinkled. He didn't look as if he had been in an accident.

"I'm okay."

"You're one fortunate man, David. That's quite a drop. It must have been a wild ride to the bottom. There are four crosses on that curve. One for each person who missed that curve and didn't live to tell about it. You're damn lucky. How did it happen?"

"I was headed for Safford and remembered I forgot something. I turned the car back to Clifton and I guess I was just going too fast around that curve."

"It must have been something important."

"Sí, muy importante—my guitarra. I left it at the Oasis. I got to have my guitarra."

"Must be special?"

"I've had that guitarra since I was eight. It was my grandpa's—he called it Paloma and taught me to play it. When he died, he left it to me. I take it everywhere. I don't know how come I forgot it this time."

As they entered Clifton, Alberto asked, "Where do you want me to drop you?"

"At the Oasis, of course. I gotta pick up Paloma."

Alberto thought it peculiar. He himself would have wanted to go straight home. The guitar must be very important indeed to the young man. Alberto made a right turn just before the Frisco River Bridge and drove to the Oasis. At least the bar wasn't too far out of his way.

In front of the bar, David opened the door and got out. "Gracias, 'mano. I really appreciate the ride. I got to have my guitarra."

The door slammed and Alberto started to back out. He looked over his shoulder to smile at David. Where had the hitchhiker gone? Except for a couple of cars parked in front of the Oasis, the parking lot behind him was empty. He rubbed his eyes. David had probably run into the building when he turned to back out. Was that possible? Alberto looked over at the mortuary next to the Oasis and a shiver went up his spine.

He didn't think about it as he drove up the winding road to the mine entrance at Plantsite. He didn't think about it while he worked. But when it was time for lunch break, he couldn't keep from talking about it to his buddies.

"Sounds like you picked up a ghost," said Anacleto Esparza.

"There's no such thing. I don't believe in ghosts."

Anacleto laughed. "This ghost's for real. Didn't you say his name was David Orozco?"

"Yeah, what of it?"

"David Orozco was killed on that curve above the river four years ago."

"You're not the only one who's given him a ride," said Tomás Calderon. "Pedro, didn't you pick up David last year?"

"¡Sí! Did he ever give me a scare! He disappeared just like that!" Pedro snapped his fingers. "I was asking him questions and it seemed like he didn't want to answer. All of a sudden, he was gone. Poof!"

"Enrique Márquez picked him up once and got him as far as the Frisco Bridge," said Anacleto. "He said the same thing."

"He goes hitchhiking the same time every month," said Tomás. "I've heard a dozen other people tell the same story. The fifteenth is when he got killed. His car was demolished at the bottom of the ravine. They had to peel it off his body. Poor family couldn't even have the casket open at the funeral."

Alberto kept shaking his head. Hard to accept, but there it was. Others had had the same experience.

"Ghosts haunt people because they want something," said Anacleto. "Maybe this David wants something. Did he tell you anything?"

"He didn't say much to me," Pedro said.

"No one gets to say much to you," Tomás said. "You like to do all the talking."

Pedro playfully punched Tomás in the arm. "Watch it, *amigo*. I'd say the same thing is true about you."

Tomás laughed.

"He told me he wanted his guitar," Alberto said. "In fact, he said it a couple of times—'I got to have my *guitarra*.'"

"They say to stop a ghost from haunting, you have to give them what they want," Anacleto said.

"Anacleto is right," Pedro said. "I propose we give David back his guitar."

"How are we gonna do that? *Por Dios*, the guy's dead," Alberto said.

"We could go talk to his family," Tomás said. "They ought to know where his guitar is. Then we can dig up his grave and bury it with him."

"What makes you think they'll believe us? People don't go digging up graves on a whim," Alberto said.

"We'll get some of the others who've given him a ride to come with us," Pedro said. "That should be proof enough to David's parents that he wants his guitar. Tomás, you talk to the other people and we'll do it next weekend. I'll call his parents and tell them we're coming to see them."

Alberto wasn't sure this was such a good plan, but if it worked, perhaps the hitchhiking mariachi would finally be laid to rest. He agreed to go with the others when they went to talk to the Orozco family.

A week later, Alberto drove to Morenci on his day off. The Orozcos lived on AC Hill and he found the place easily. Several cars and trucks were parked alongside the road in front of a large two-story frame house. A dozen men were gathered next to Pedro's pickup. They were recalling their stories about the hitchhiker.

"¡*Silencios*! We can't all talk at once," Pablo said. "When we go in, let Tomás do the talking and the rest of us will tell what we saw."

Tomás led the group toward the house and knocked on the door. Alberto trailed behind them, still not sure this was the right thing to do. *Señora* Orozco invited them into the *sala* and gestured to the chairs that had been set up around the room. *Señor* Orozco was sitting on a worn leather armchair and *la señora* sat next to him. The men found places on the sofa and the surrounding chairs.

Tomás cleared his throat. "*Señor y Señora* Orozco, we have come here today because of your son, David. Since his accident four years ago, these men have seen and talked to your son."

"*Sí*, we have heard rumors that our son's ghost has appeared, but we did not believe them," said *Señor* Orozco.

"We do not come with rumors, *señor*. These men will tell you what happened to them."

Each man spoke in turn, telling their story about how David appeared on the curve and how they gave him a ride only to have him disappear. Some said he was in their car for a few minutes, others that they had driven him as far as the Oasis.

By the time it was Alberto's turn, he believed that the parents had to be convinced to bury the guitar with David. He told about his experience with their son's ghost.

"I think that your son wants Paloma, the guitar his grandfather gave him," Alberto said at the end of his story. "A couple of times on our trip into Clifton, he told me, 'I got to have my *guitarra*.' I've heard ghosts haunt people because they want something. When they get what they want, they rest in peace. *Por favor*, can we give David his guitar?"

Tears streamed down *Señora* Orozco's cheeks. *Señor* Orozco patted her hand. Alberto felt sorry for them.

"*Gracias, muchachos*, for telling us about our son," *Señor* Orozco said. "On the night he died, David forgot his guitar at the Oasis. If he had not gone back to get it, he would not have had the accident."

"I believe that giving ghosts what they want gives them peace," said *Señora* Orozco. "We want our son to rest in peace. Let me get David's *guitarra* and we will all go to *el cemeterio* to take it to him."

"I will call the *padre* to meet us there," said *Señor* Orozco.

At the cemetery, Alberto took his turn digging with the other men. His shovel struck something hard. He scraped the last bit of dirt off the casket and climbed out of the grave. *Señor* Orozco opened the guitar case and the priest blessed it with holy water and a prayer. A couple of men pried the casket open.

Señor Orozco handed the guitar to Alberto. "I think David would like it if you gave him his guitar," he said.

The guitar was a beauty. No wonder David had wanted it so badly. The antique wood gleamed in the sunlight. Alberto caressed the smooth wood and his hand plucked a string, the soft note resonating over the cemetery. Alberto placed the guitar on the bones that were dressed in a tattered mariachi costume. The priest recited a closing prayer and the men shoveled dirt back onto the closed casket. Afterward, they all filed back to their cars in silence.

A month later, Alberto was on graveyard shift again. He was driving toward the infamous curve and slowed down as usual. A man in a Mexican sombrero was hitching a ride next to the four crosses. Alberto stopped. It was David! The young mariachi stood at the side of the road clutching his guitar. He smiled and touched the brim of his hat before he disappeared. Alberto knew this was the last time anyone would see the hitchhiking ghost. He and his friends had done the right thing. At long last, David was at peace.

BLESS ME, FATHER

Lupe Santos pulled back the maroon curtain and went into the confessional. She knelt on the hard wooden kneeler and crossed herself. "Bless me, father, for I have sinned. It's been a week since my last confession." Lupe confessed she had told her mother a couple of white lies and had a fight with her younger sister.

"For your penance, say one Our Father and three Hail Marys." The words, spoken in a thick accent, surprised Lupe. She had expected Father Maloney. This must be the new priest—the one coming from Ireland. She wasn't pleased with the penance he gave her. Father Maloney would have given her at least three times as much.

Lupe recited the Act of Contrition as the priest requested, received absolution for her sins, and left the confessional. She marched up the aisle to kneel in front of *la Virgen de Guadalupe*, next to her best friend, Clotilde Rodríguez. It irked her that the penance had not been more.

Already angry with the new priest, she thought, and she hadn't even met him face-to-face. Her mother's words came back to haunt her. "What kind of nun will you be with that temper?" Chagrined, she took out her beads and started to pray.

"Lupe, if you're going to pray a rosary, I'm not waiting for you." Clotilde, or Tillie as she preferred to be called, leaned over and whispered in her ear. "I can't believe you had that many sins—you're always so good!"

"Shh! I have to. I got angry with the new priest because he didn't give me a harsh enough penance. I've got to make up for it."

"That's punishing yourself—it doesn't count. Why don't you go back in and tell him? He'll probably give you less than a rosary. Anyway, I'd go back—he sounds so sexy with that Irish accent."

"Tillie, how can you say that in church?" Lupe pushed her friend away.

"Because it's true!" Tillie giggled and tugged Lupe's long, black braid. "I'll wait for you outside, kiddo. This kneeling is killing my knees."

Lupe shook her head. Tillie acted like a scatterbrain, but she was one of the smartest students at Morenci High. After graduation next year, she planned to go to the University of Arizona to study engineering. Those male engineering students would surely be in for a surprise. Tillie's appearance and behavior, such a contrast to Lupe's own, were deceiving. No one would expect the petite girl with her short, sandy curls and green eyes to be a super brain. Lupe chuckled and put the rosary back into her pocket. She could say it before she went to bed tonight. Genuflecting before the main altar, she went out to her friend.

"That was quick," Tillie said. "You must tell me your secret for speeding through a rosary."

Lupe tapped Tillie on the arm. "How you love to tease me."

Tillie grinned up at Lupe who was a couple of inches taller. "You're always so serious—you need me to spice up your life."

"You're right. The only time I get into trouble is with you." Lupe started walking down the stairs.

"Trouble? Girl, you should know the meaning of trouble." Tillie followed Lupe down the hill. "Honestly, you're much too serious. Remember, aspiring nuns can still have a little fun. It's our senior year in high school—live a little! Go out on a date. Half the boys in our class are dying to go out with you. God, what I wouldn't do for your high cheekbones and gorgeous hair—all that rippling, long black hair that's going to get chopped off."

"I only grew it long so I can sacrifice it when I take my vows," Lupe said.

"Come on, admit it, girl—it's your one vanity!" Tillie put her arm through Lupe's.

"You're right." Lupe laughed. "That's why it'll be such a good sacrifice." The two girls headed home.

Sunday morning Lupe arose with the sun and walked down the hill to Holy Cross Church for early Mass. She preferred it to the ten o'clock service because it was simpler. The choir didn't sing and people weren't decked out in their finest clothes. There was nothing to distract from the Mass. She wished she could convince her family to get up early and come with her, but they preferred to sleep in and go later.

Lupe crossed herself with holy water as she entered the church and genuflected in the aisle before going into her accustomed pew. It was in the middle of the church and her favorite. She could gaze at the stained-glass window of Saint Theresa in her Carmelite habit. Lupe knelt and prayed.

As usual, her thoughts wandered as she prayed. Next year at this time, she'd be on her way to Oklahoma City to enter the Carmelite convent her cousin Socorro had joined four years ago. She contemplated the stained-glass image of Saint Theresa. Socorro had sent her a picture of herself in a similar nun's habit, and Lupe imagined how she would look dressed the same way.

Her reverie was interrupted as the other parishioners stood up around her. As Lupe sprang to her feet, Tillie tiptoed into the pew, half-genuflected and stood beside her.

"Whew, I made it!"

"Shh! Mass is starting." Tillie's behavior in church was exasperating to Lupe. Sometimes she wished her madcap friend would go to the later Mass.

The new priest walked up to the ornate altar. The Latin prayers, intoned in a rich baritone with an Irish accent, dis-

tracted Lupe. They sounded so different from the way Father
Maloney said them with his flat midwestern accent. The congregation stood to hear the gospel read in English and then
sat to hear the new priest's sermon.

His hands shook as he brought out a sheaf of papers from
under the pulpit. He adjusted the microphone to his height.

"Good morn..." The microphone screeched and the priest
fumbled to adjust it. "Sorry about that. Good morning. I'm the
new assistant pastor, Father Patrick O'Donnell." His voice
sounded flat as if he were reading. "This is my first parish and
I'm happy to be here. I'm from Ireland and this is my first
time in your country. Please be patient with me as I learn
your customs."

Lupe studied the priest as he stammered through the sermon, which he read in a monotone. He was tall—taller than
anyone she had ever met before. He had to be over six feet
tall. And young—she hadn't expected a priest so young. Black
hair slicked back from a wide forehead was a sharp contrast to
his fair complexion. A beak-like nose lent a rugged look to otherwise patrician features.

"Isn't he handsome?" Tillie sighed and poked Lupe's side.
"Why does he have to be a priest?"

"Tillie! Be quiet. How many times do I have to tell you."
He was not at all what Lupe thought a priest should look like.
She found herself disliking him on sight for that reason alone.

Father O'Donnell had moved on to parish announce-
ments. He read a letter from Taylor Dunne. The mining company was giving Holy Cross Church notice that the church
had to be torn down by the following year. A piece of land in
Plantsite had been allocated by T.D. for the new church. Lupe
listened to the whispers around her. She could tell the parishioners were upset by the news.

"My parents got a notice, too." Tillie confided in Lupe's
ear.

"Oh, no, this is the second time your family's had to
move."

"It's okay with them. My dad's retiring and they planned to move to Phoenix anyway."

After Mass, Lupe and Tillie went around to the various groups gathered outside the church and listened to the people's concerns about T.D.'s notice.

"T.D. giveth and T.D. taketh away," Mr. Nuñez said.

"But it's not fair. Our homes are here. I don't want to move," Mrs. Jimenez said. "My grandfather built our house."

"It may not be fair, but T.D. does what it wants," Mr. Fernández said. "They own all the land—they own Morenci. I had to tear down my house last year and move to Plantsite. I hated to do it, but I had to. My job depended on it."

"Surely the company isn't going to destroy the whole town?" Mrs. Fernández asked. "They haven't announced they would."

"Not officially," Mr. Nuñez said. "But giving notice to the church is pretty strong indication that's what's going to happen. Every week more families are getting a letter from T.D."

Most of the conversations followed the same vein and Lucy detected a sense of helplessness. No one in her family had yet been asked to tear down their house so it didn't affect her personally, but she was upset about the church.

"How can they make people tear down their church?" Lupe asked Tillie as they walked home. "Those beautiful stained-glass windows—the altar...what will happen to them?"

"Probably be moved to the new church."

"It won't be the same." Lupe grimaced and Tillie nudged her.

"You just don't like change. It can be for the good, you know."

"I don't see how destroying Morenci can be good change."

"Look at the bright side—everything will be new and besides we're both leaving here. I can hardly wait."

"But we won't have a hometown to come back to."

"You think those nuns will let you come back? I don't plan to come back anyway."

By this time the girls had reached Tillie's house and they parted company. Lupe climbed AC Hill to her house. So many changes—a new priest, houses being torn down, the church, maybe the whole town. Tillie was right. She didn't like change, especially when she didn't see any good in it.

As the weeks passed the young priest assumed his parish duties and Lupe found she couldn't agree with him on anything. He was in charge of the catechism classes and the Catholic Youth Organization. Lupe taught catechism and had done so for four years. She resented any recommendations Father O'Donnell made and, as president of the CYO, she disapproved of any activities he suggested.

The more she argued with him and criticized his sermons, the harder he tried to win her over. He asked her opinion of everything and listened intently to her answers. She found herself enjoying their discussions as she struggled to come up with logical arguments for her sometimes illogical positions.

The other teen-agers, however, extolled his virtues. "Father Pat this, and Father Pat that." Lupe never called him anything but Father O'Donnell. It bothered her that Tillie and all her other girlfriends had crushes on the young priest. The boys were won over by his athletic ability. He didn't wear his Roman collar during CYO activities and this irritated Lupe even more. Priests should not behave like this one did.

As the months passed, however, Lupe softened. She noticed Father O'Donnell's patience in dealing with her behavior. One Sunday after the late Mass, which Lupe had started attending with her family since Father O'Donnell gave the early one, she found him outside greeting parishioners as they left the church.

"This lass has been wonderful, Mr. and Mrs. Santos. She, more than anyone else, has helped me to learn about your country."

"Thank you, Father, we're very proud of her." Mr. Santos shook the priest's proffered hand. "She's going to the convent next year to become a nun like her cousin."

"Yes, I heard." Father put his hands on Lupe's shoulders and she felt their heat seep through her body. "I've been wondering something—that statue of the Virgin Mary on the altar…"

"I know what you're going to ask, Father." Mr. Santos nodded his head and chuckled. "That statue looks like Lupita because my grandfather, Diego Santos, carved it. His model was my sainted mother when she was young. Lupita looks just like her."

"Your grandfather was a master craftsman." The priest smiled at Lupe as she looked up over her shoulder at him.

"Sí, he was. He came from New Mexico—from a long line of wood carvers." Mr. Santos squared his shoulders and stood a little taller. "Our ancestors had been carving saints there long before the English settled their colonies on the east coast. Santos, our last name, probably came from that."

"I'm struck by the depiction of our Holy Mother—the olive skin, black hair, and draping are very unusual."

"It's our Mexican version of the Virgin—*la Virgen de Guadalupe*," Lupe said. "She appeared to an Indian named Juan Diego in Mexico and imprinted her image on his *ayate*."

"Lupe is named for *la Virgen de Guadalupe*," said Mrs. Santos.

Father O'Donnell thanked the Santos family for sharing the story and turned to the next family waiting to greet him. As Lupe walked to the car, she felt the lingering warmth of his hands on her shoulders. His touch had thrilled her more than his compliments.

One evening in March, seven months after Father O'Donnell's arrival in Morenci, Lupe attended a CYO meeting that changed her opinion of him. He tried to present the lesson, but he was distracted.

"I think I'll dispense with the lesson tonight," he said. "I received some bad news from home that I'd like to share with you, but first I have to tell you a bit about the history of Ireland."

For the next hour, Lupe did not take her eyes off Father O'Donnell's face. His passion as he spoke of the historical struggle Catholics had waged to gain control of their country made her heart ache. It reminded her of the discrimination Mexicans suffered in Morenci and how T.D. had the power to control their lives.

His eyes welled with tears when he announced that his childhood best friend had been killed in an exchange of gunfire between Catholics and Protestants. Lupe sat in silence as the other teen-agers asked Father O'Donnell questions. After the meeting ended and the others left, she approached him.

"Father, I'm so sorry about your friend. I'll remember him in my prayers." She put her hand out and he engulfed it in both of his.

"Thank you, Lupe."

She felt a pleasant sensation radiating up her arm from his touch. Shocked, she pulled her hand out of his grasp.

"I've...I've got to get home." Lupe pulled her hand away. "Good night Father." She turned and ran up the basement stairs, her waist-length hair swishing behind her.

When she reached the front of the church, Tillie came up to her. "Where were you? I thought you were right behind me."

"I stopped to speak with Father Pat," Lupe said.

"I wish I had thought of that. He looked so sad—like he needed comforting. Did you hug him? I would have."

"Tillie!"

"Just kidding—don't get upset. But I bet he probably would have appreciated a hug." Tillie took Lupe's hand and they walked off into the darkness.

That night in bed after she said her prayers, Lupe remembered how she felt when Father O'Donnell touched her hand. She had never felt that way before. When Lupe was ten years old, her cousin Socorro told her she was planning to become a nun. Lupe had always admired the nuns who came each year to teach summer catechism, but she never realized until then that she, too, could someday be a nun. When Socorro graduated from high school, she left Morenci to enter the Carmelite order. She wrote to Lupe often, encouraging her to follow in her footsteps. As a result, Lupe didn't go through the boy-crazy stage most of her friends did. She didn't date and although many of her friends were boys, none of them made her feel the way Father O'Donnell did. How could she feel that way about a priest? She reached for the rosary hanging on the headboard and fell asleep praying.

As the weeks passed, Lupe tried to avoid Father O'Donnell, but it was difficult because her after-school life revolved around the church. She no longer daydreamed about herself as a nun—instead she had to stop herself from thinking about Father O'Donnell's blue eyes. They were as brilliant as the Arizona sky. And his smile warmed her insides. The Irish accent she had been so critical of when he first arrived, now seemed charming. She began to call him Father Pat in front of others, but when she thought about him it was "Patrick."

When she brushed her teeth before going to bed at night, she caught herself staring at the rectory out the bathroom window. A rectangle of light shone from his bedroom, and she wondered what he was doing. In bed, she found herself having to say a rosary, sometimes two—just to stop thinking about him.

Two weeks after graduation, the youth group rented the Morenci pool for an evening swimming party. Lupe saw Father Pat standing at the edge of the pool. She swam up to him.

"Hi, Father."

"Hi, Lupe, how's the water?"

"Nice and cool."

Lupe wiped beads of water off her face and looked up into Father Pat's eyes as he squatted to put his hand in the pool. Their eyes locked. Lupe felt as if a charge of electricity had zapped her. No words were exchanged, but at that moment she knew he felt the same way. His hand reached out to her cheek, but before he could touch it, she ducked into the water and swam to the opposite side of the pool. She pulled herself out of the water and rushed into the dressing room.

He was a priest. All she wanted was to be a nun—didn't she? Confused, she tore off her wet bathing suit and cap, toweled dry and threw on her Bermuda shorts and T-shirt. She ran out the door and didn't stop running until she found herself in front of the church.

Lupe thought about going in and begging forgiveness, but she couldn't bring herself to do it. She loved him—how could she say she was sorry for that? How could she stop loving him? Maybe it would happen over time or maybe...no, she didn't want to think about that. Lupe turned her back on the church and went home to bed.

For the first time, she didn't pray her rosary. She fell asleep and dreamed she was dressed in a bridal gown and veil, surrounded by nuns. They were leading her up to the altar to become a bride of Christ. When they reached the altar, she saw the priest was Patrick in elaborate vestments. In front of him was a bridegroom with his back to her. When he turned to face her, Lupe saw it was Patrick in a tuxedo. He reached for her hand and pulled her to his side. Patrick, the priest, performed the marriage ceremony. When Patrick, the bridegroom, put the ring on Lupe's finger, the nuns clapped.

Priest Patrick took one of Lupe's hands and bridegroom Patrick the other. They propelled her down the aisle, out of the church. Townspeople waited outside and instead of flinging rice at them, they pelted them with stones. Both Patricks disappeared and Lupe found herself in the midst of the jeering crowd. Blood from wounds on her head and arms dripped on the white satin gown. She screamed. Lupe woke up in a cold sweat. She grabbed her rosary and knelt on the side of the bed and prayed to *la Virgen de Guadalupe* for help.

The next day, Lupe started her summer job at the church. Father Maloney had requested help in reorganizing the church records. Lupe, Tillie, and their friends, Catalina Huerta and Amanda Jiménez, had volunteered.

"Come on in, *muchachas*." Father Maloney led them into the rectory living room. "As you can see, Father Pat set everything up for you this morning before he left to play golf. It's his day off."

Lupe was glad Patrick wasn't there. Father Maloney instructed the girls on what he wanted done and she concentrated on what he was saying. The project sounded easy and it would be fun to work with her friends.

"Take a break at noon and go down to the Longfellow Inn for lunch. Order anything you want and have them put it on my tab," Father said. "It's the least we can do to repay you for your help. By the way, are you girls interested in classical music?"

Not waiting for an answer, he rubbed his hands together like a small boy about to spring a surprise. He turned to the bottom shelf of the bookcase and selected one of the many records.

"This is Debussy's *La Mer*." He placed the record on the hi-fi turntable and strains of beautiful music filled the room. "I have Bach, Beethoven, Mozart, and more. You're welcome to listen to the entire collection as you work." He smiled and left the room.

The girls worked on organizing the church records until the music stopped. Lupe selected a new recording and placed it on the turntable.

"My family just got a letter from T.D." Amanda said as Beethoven's Fifth started. "We have to tear down our house. My mom is really upset."

"We got one, too," Catalina said. "My folks don't like the idea much, but I think it's great! Oscar's put in for one of those new T.D. houses they're building in Plantsite and he got one. We'll be able to move in after our wedding next month."

"But what about your parents?" Lupe asked.

"That's the best part. They're going to put in for a new house, too—so hopefully it'll be next to ours. Oscar's parents already live in Plantsite."

The changes that were happening in Morenci occupied the girls' conversation for the next hour. Lupe was perturbed because her grandparents lived a few houses away from Amanda's. She wondered if they had gotten a notice, too. If they had to leave Morenci, they couldn't get a company house because her grandfather had retired years ago. They'd have to live with one of their children. Lupe sighed and wished her friends would change the subject.

When Lupe went to the bathroom a couple of hours later, she passed Father Pat's room. The door was ajar. Curiosity got the best of her. She pushed it open and peeked in. So this was the room she had been staring at every night. A single bed topped with a white chenille bedspread was squeezed against the wall. A crucifix, hung over the metal headboard, was the only decoration on the bare walls.

Lupe stole a glance over her shoulder and was in the room before she could stop herself. The door swung closed behind her. An old dresser opposite the bed had a comb and brush set, some toiletries, and a framed photograph on its battered top. She picked up the photo. It was of Patrick's family. His smiling mother stood in the middle surrounded by four young men and three young women. Patrick and one of his brothers, who looked older than he, wore Roman collars. One of the women was in a nun's habit.

Lupe put down the picture as if it had burned her and turned to leave. Patrick's black cassock hung on a hook on the door. On impulse, she gathered the garment in her arms and buried her face in it. She inhaled Patrick's scent and ached to have his arms around her. Turning her back to the door, she enveloped herself with the cassock's long sleeves. What was she doing? She dropped the sleeves and hurried from the room.

The days that followed seemed to fly. The girls took turns selecting the records and announcing the composers. It wasn't long before Lupe found she could identify a musical piece from its opening notes. Patrick's duties took him out of the parish house, so she was grateful she didn't have to see him. When he was in the office, however, she avoided his eyes.

One Saturday, a couple of weeks after Lupe started working at the rectory, the CYO sponsored an evening bonfire and wiener roast. After helping to load the station wagon with supplies, Lupe found herself squeezed into the front seat with two of her friends. Father Pat was driving and she was sitting next to him—so close they could have been joined from shoulder to knee. Lupe felt as if her left side was on fire. It spread to the rest of her body and she was glad it was dark so no one could see her flushed face. She tried to scoot closer to Tillie.

"Father Pat, did you ever go on a wiener roast when you were a teen-ager?" Tillie wiggled in the front seat, pushing Lupe nearer to Patrick.

"No...lots of bonfires though."

"Did you take your girlfriend?" Tillie poked Lupe in the ribs.

"I've never had a girlfriend."

"Why not?" asked Amanda from the other side of Tillie.

"I attended a boy's school. It was always understood I was going to the seminary like my older brother James. I never had the chance to meet any girls." Father O'Donnell downshifted on the curvy road and Lupe felt his muscles tense as he moved his leg.

SUFFER SMOKE

"It must have been pretty boring going to school with just guys," Jimmy Cisneros said from the back seat.

"Not too bad. Sports and other activities kept us busy when we weren't studying."

"What kind of sports did you play?"

"Soccer and boxing. As a matter of fact, that's how I broke my nose." Father Pat rubbed his nose. "I was fighting for the middleweight championship when I got knocked out."

"What else did you do to keep busy, Father Pat?" asked Catalina.

"I played the saxophone."

"That's cool," said Tiny López. "I play the guitar. What kind of music do you like?"

"Jazz. We used to have a jazz band in the seminary."

"That's Lupe's favorite music," said Tillie. "She has a bunch of scratchy old jazz records her uncle left her."

The conversation turned to other topics as they drove down the dirt road in the moonlight. Lupe was silent the entire trip. When they arrived at Eagle Creek, the teens piled out of the station wagon. Four more cars pulled up beside them and unloaded other CYO members. They unpacked the cars and started a big fire.

Lupe was glad so many of her friends had come. The class of 1966. It seemed as though they had just started kindergarten and now they had graduated. This summer would be over much too soon and it would be time for her to leave. She studied her friends' faces as they sat by the fire roasting hot dogs. Others would be leaving even sooner. Jimmy, Tiny, and Saul had been drafted and were reporting for basic training next week. They'd probably get sent to Vietnam right after that. Tillie and a couple of other girls were starting college in the fall. Catalina was marrying Oscar Fernández next month. Friends she grew up with—all going their separate ways. The church and people's homes were being torn down. Too many changes were happening all at once.

"Penny for your thoughts." Father Pat plopped down on the log next to her.

"I was just thinking about how hard it's going to be to say goodbye to my friends."

"I know how you feel. After we were ordained, my friends and I were sent in different directions."

"You're really far from your people. I bet you miss them."

"I do—when I'm not busy. Being a priest is not quite what I thought it would be. It's a lonely life. Ah, but you don't want to hear about that. Tell me, lass, what jazz records do you have?"

"I've got all the greats—Duke Ellington, Cab Calloway, Louis Armstrong, Count Basie, Woody Herman, and singers like Bessie Smith, Billie Holiday, Lena Horne, and Ella Fitzgerald. All in original 78's. They range from the late 20's to the 40's."

"I'm impressed. How did you come by such a collection?"

"My father found them in his uncle's house when they were cleaning it out after he died. I also have an old Victrola I play them on."

"Who's your favorite singer?"

"Billie Holiday, hands down! No one sings the blues like she does."

"You're right—she's my favorite also. When Lady Day sings, she sounds like a whole orchestra. I can hear the soft wail of a saxophone, then the piercing blast of a trumpet. Her voice seems to creep right under your skin and stay there," Patrick said.

"I think she sings from the depths of her soul. Sometimes I feel as if she's having a heart-to-heart talk with me. She..."

"Hey, you guys, here's some sticks. Let's go roast some marshmallows." Tillie handed Father Pat the sticks and pulled Lupe off the log

Lupe resented Tillie's interruption—she was enjoying her talk with Patrick about jazz. Her friends were all into rock 'n

roll so there was no one with whom she could share her inter-
est.

When they loaded up the cars to leave the picnic site,
Lupe made sure she was again sitting next to Patrick. This
time, she didn't care when she was pushed against him. His
body felt pleasurable next to hers and the sensation, although
disturbing, was also thrilling. She pretended he wasn't a
priest. Tillie started to sing "Blueberry Hill" and everyone
joined in. They sang songs the rest of the way to the parish
house and Lupe enjoyed every minute.

After the station wagon was unloaded, Lupe and Tillie
were the only ones left. They were in Tillie's car when Father
Pat came and tapped on the passenger's window. Lupe rolled
it down.

"I was just wondering if perhaps you and Tillie could
come by next Monday evening and bring some of your jazz
records and the Victrola. I'd love to hear the original cuts on
an old phonograph. You could listen to some of my collection."

"Not me, Father," Tillie said. "I'm not into that music.
Besides, I have a movie date with Tiny."

"I'll be happy to come. Thanks, Father Pat. Good night!"
Lupe rolled up the window and Tillie backed the car out of the
driveway.

"You got a hot date with Father Pat!"

"It's not a date. We both enjoy listening to jazz and he
wants to..."

"Kiss you, hug you, make mad passionate love to you..."

"Tillie! It's not that. He's a priest, for God's sake." Lupe
wished she could think of something to change the topic.

"Come on, Lupe, spill the beans to your dearest friend.
Doesn't he turn you on just a little bit? He's the best-looking
guy in town. We all have crushes on him and it's okay."

"Okay? Okay to have a crush on a priest?"

"Lupe, you're such a prude. Of course it's okay because it's
not going anywhere. It just makes for some nice daydreams."

SUFFER SMOKE

Tillie maneuvered the car around the curve where an old dance hall had once stood.

"Remember *El Imperio*?" At last Lupe had a different subject. "Didn't your father help tear it down?"

"Yeah. He took out the oak floor and put it in our living room. Sometimes when I'm in there alone, I can almost hear dancers *tapatiando* to Mexican music."

"Probably a bunch of ghosts." Lupe looked around the hills comprising Morenci. "So many houses are being torn down. My grandparents have to vacate their house in a couple of months. They're moving in with my uncle."

"Eventually the whole town will be gone, but we won't be here so why worry? Here's your house. See you tomorrow at Mass?"

"Sure, 'night." Lupe got out of the car and watched Tillie drive down the road toward her house.

As she brushed her teeth that night, Lupe stared out the window at the rectangle of light shining from Patrick's room. So Tillie thought it was okay to have a crush on a priest. Maybe it was. She had a crush on Patrick and that was all. She'd get over it before she left for the convent. In the meantime, she would enjoy his company.

On Monday evening after dinner, Lupe loaded the family car with the Victrola and a box full of her favorite records. Patrick helped her unload them when she got to the rectory.

"Where's Father Maloney?" Lupe asked after going into the living room.

"He got called away to a meeting with the Bishop in Tucson. He probably won't be back until after midnight." Patrick set the phonograph on the coffee table. "This is a beauty."

"It's a little more work than a hi-fi, but the sound is incredible. You feel like you're back in those days. What do you want to hear first?"

"How about this Louis Armstrong." Patrick held up a record. "I've never heard him play with King Oliver's Creole Jazz Band."

"That's a good one. It was when he was first starting out. He played second horn to Joe Oliver and they were great together." Lupe cranked the phonograph and Patrick placed the needle on the record.

The driving jazz blared out—so different from the classical music Lupe had been listening to earlier that morning in this same room. Patrick sat on the large leather armchair in the corner of the room and kept time with his foot. Lupe slipped to the floor and swayed with the music. When "Canal Street Blues" came on with King Joe's and Satchmo's trumpets, Patrick smiled and Lupe couldn't resist getting up to dance with the music. Patrick clapped when it was over and Lupe collapsed on the floor giggling.

"You were wonderful! You're a great dancer."

"Not really, I just make it up as the music sweeps me along. Let's hear one of your records."

"How about Cab Calloway? I like his 'Hi De Ho Man' and 'Minnie, the Moocher.'" Patrick cranked the Victrola and put the needle on the record. He sang the words along as the record played and Lupe joined him.

Lupe was having fun. They played a dozen records before she put on Billie Holiday. It was as though she had been saving the best for last. The rich mellow voice singing "Solitude" reached into the secret places of Lupe's heart. It tore at her very nerve endings. Lady Day's singing led Lupe down a lonely road she didn't know existed within herself. She shivered and glanced up at Patrick. Tears were flowing down his cheeks. He leaned forward and put his face in his hands. Lupe didn't know what to do at first—he seemed to be filled with the very despair Billie Holiday described in her song. She couldn't let him sit there so alone—she had to comfort him. She crawled over and encircled him with her arms. He gathered her long hair and buried his face in it, wiping away the tears.

"Your hair smells so sweet—like fresh peaches. Lupe, I'm..." He turned Lupe's face toward him and caressed her cheek. His hand lifted her chin and he kissed her—gently at first, then with passion. Patrick's kisses aroused all the emotions Lupe had stored up the past few months. She returned his kisses with ardor and didn't notice when they tumbled to the floor as Billie sang the words, "God bless the child that's got his own." Lady Day's sultry voice was like honey, blessing their lovemaking.

Lupe basked in Patrick's admiration as he stroked her body afterwards. It was as if he were memorizing it with his fingertips. The clock in the office next door struck ten.

"Patrick, I've got to get home." Lupe grabbed her clothes and started dressing. She peeked at Patrick's smooth muscular back as he dressed. He was so beautiful—she wished she could stay with him forever. Oh God, what had they done? This was wrong, so wrong.

"Lupe what's the matter?" Patrick cupped her face in his hands and tilted it up to his.

"I..." What could she say to him—how? "I...I feel so guilty. What we did isn't right, is it?" Tears sprang to her eyes.

"Don't feel like that. It is right." Patrick clasped her hands in both of his and kissed them. "I love you. That makes it right."

"But...but you're a priest!" Lupe didn't mean to blurt it out so accusingly.

"I'm not cut out to be a priest. I've been so lonely here—you're the only bright spot in my life." He embraced her and kissed her lips. "I've been thinking about leaving the priesthood. I want to get married, have a family...I want to marry you."

"No...no, we can't." Lupe pushed him away. "We'll be excommunicated. I couldn't live with that." She ran out of the house and got into the car without looking back. That night as she brushed her teeth, she resisted the impulse to look out the bathroom window at Patrick's window. From now on, she would have to stay away from Patrick. She crawled into bed with her rosary and prayed for strength.

≋

In the darkness of the church that same night, salty tears ran down the wooden cheeks of the statue of *la Virgen de Guadalupe*. The next morning, Lourdes Delgado, one of the old crones who attended daily Mass, was saying her rosary at the foot of *la Virgen* after Mass. When she finished, she crossed herself and kissed the crucifix on her rosary. She looked up and saw crystals on the statue's cheeks. It looked to her as if the statue had been crying.

"¡*Padre Maloney, venga aquí!*" When the priest didn't come, she ran into the sacristy where he was putting away his vestments. The old woman grabbed his hand. "Come see the miracle! *La virgen* is shedding tears!"

The priest had no choice but to follow the hysterical woman to the altar on the right side of the church.

"Look...there on her cheeks..."

"What? *Señora* Delgado, I don't see anything."

"*Sí*, tears...on her cheeks." The old lady peered up but didn't see what she had seen earlier. "Maybe it's the light...here, kneel with me, you'll see. There!" She pointed at the statue. "See *Padre*...see the tears!"

"I see some crystals, but there aren't any tears."

"Dried tears, *Padre*. Look how they come from her eyes. *La virgen* has cried. *La virgen* is giving us a sign. She doesn't want the church to be torn down. ¡*Es un milagro!*"

"No, *Señora* Delgado. The statue is made of wood, probably some moisture is seeping out. It's not a miracle." The priest helped the old woman to her feet. "I'll get a ladder and clean her face. You'll see it's nothing."

The priest wiped the last traces of crystals from the statue's cheeks with a wet cloth. "See, it washed off. Don't go getting everybody all excited about miracles."

"*Bueno, Padre*. But I'm going to check her every morning from now on." Lourdes crossed herself, genuflected in front of the main altar and limped down the aisle. At the church doors, she dipped her hand in holy water and turned to look in awe at the statue before she made the sign of the cross and left the church.

Father Maloney studied the statue as he wiped the dust off. There didn't appear to be encrustations anywhere else. He hoped *Señora* Delgado kept it to herself. He didn't need the congregation to get fired up about miracles. It was going to be difficult enough getting them to tear the church down and come up with the money to build a new one.

He looked around the church and shook his head. It had survived all these years—maybe not the same building, but a Catholic church had stood on this same ground for over eighty-five years. The original church had been destroyed by successive dynamite blasts within a three-month period in 1913. No one knew who did it, but people suspected it was done because anti-Catholic and anti-Mexican feelings were rampant in Morenci in those days. The people had rebuilt their church, undaunted by the bombings or threats against the priests' lives. Now the church was to be destroyed again, not to be rebuilt on the same site.

These walls contained so many memories for the Mexican people of Morenci...generations had been married here, had baptized their children here, had watched their children receive their First Holy Communion, and had been confirmed soldiers of Christ. And, of course, the funerals. Soon, all too soon, it would all be gone. Father Maloney felt protective of his flock of more than 800 families, but there was nothing he could do. He shook his head. No, nothing would stop T.D. from expanding its mining operation into the town—no matter how much he prayed.

In the days that followed, Lupe did her work at the parish house and avoided being alone with Patrick. She could feel his eyes boring into her—sending her messages. If only things were different. If only he weren't a priest. Lupe loved him with her whole being, but she couldn't steal him away from the church. She could never love anyone the way she loved Patrick. Since she couldn't have him, she decided to go ahead with her plan to go into the convent. There was only one thing she had to do to get back into God's good graces—go to confession.

It took many more days for Lupe to get enough courage to finally enter the confessional. She went to Father Maloney instead of Patrick.

"Bless me, Father, for I have sinned." Lupe recited a list of minor indiscretions since her last confession. "Father, I have a large sin to confess—it's very difficult for me to say it."

"It's all right, my child. Just go ahead and let it out."

"I...I made love with a man and I'm not married."

Father Maloney gave her a long lecture about sex outside of marriage, but in the end, he gave her absolution and her penance was a week of rosaries. It seemed as if a great weight had been lifted off Lupe. She was forgiven. It would never happen again. Not until after leaving the church did Lupe realize she had failed to say it was a priest she had sex with. Did the absolution still count? It bothered her, but she decided to say an extra rosary each day to make up for her oversight.

During the first part of July, Lupe spent her spare time with her friends getting ready for Catalina's wedding. She was one of the bridesmaids along with Tillie and ten other girls. Lupe was so preoccupied with work at the parish house and plans for the wedding, she didn't notice she missed her period. The wedding and her job were both over by mid-July. But then the Sisters of Charity came to Morenci to run the summer catechism classes so Lupe was caught up with planning lessons for her fourth-grade class. In the evenings, she attended the teen catechism class taught by Patrick and the three nuns.

One of the nuns, Sister Eleanor, was tall and attractive. It seemed to Lupe that every time she saw Patrick nowadays,

Sister Eleanor was walking alongside him in deep conversation. One evening, she and Tillie followed them to the parish hall where the classes were being taught.

"Their habits make them look like crows," Lupe said in a low voice.

"What?" Tillie put out her hand and stopped Lupe in her tracks. "Did I just hear that come out of Miss Goody-Two-Shoes' mouth?"

"Well, they do. Look at her. That long black gown and that ridiculous bonnet. And the way she looks up at Father Pat—it's sickening!"

"Do I detect a touch of jealousy here, my dear?"

"No, I'm not jealous. Why should I be jealous?"

"Why indeed? Absolutely no reason—except, perhaps you have a crush on Father Pat?"

"Of course not. If anyone has a crush on him, it's Sister Eleanor. Nuns shouldn't behave that way. Look at her giggling like a schoolgirl."

"Why should she be different, she's only human like the rest of us. Father Pat has that effect on all females. Jesus, is he ever gorgeous, and the best part is, he doesn't know it!"

"Tillie, I don't feel like going to class tonight—you go on without me." Lupe's stomach lurched and she felt nauseated. She retched.

"What's the matter, kiddo? Do you feel sick?" Tillie felt Lupe's forehead.

"I think maybe I'm coming down with the flu. I'd better go home."

"Forget class, I'll walk you home. Come on." Tillie put an arm around Lupe's waist and they walked back the way they had come.

It was difficult for Lupe to watch Sister Eleanor steal so much of Patrick's time, but it was just as well. His attention was diverted elsewhere and it gave her a chance to try to get over her feelings for him. But by the third week in August, summer catechism was over and the Sisters of Charity left

Morenci. Lupe was glad. Now she had no reason to see Patrick outside of daily Mass.

One morning she woke up feeling nauseated again, and she ran to the bathroom to throw up. Suddenly, she remembered her Aunt Rosa's pregnancy. Oh, no! It couldn't be. She rushed to the calendar on her desk. There were no marks for her period last month and she was a week overdue this month. No! How could this happen?

Lupe sat on the edge of her bed. She couldn't become a nun if she was going to be a mother. It wasn't fair—only one time and her whole life was ruined. Her parents would never forgive her. She didn't know what to do—maybe Patrick had an idea. Tomorrow she would go to confession and wait until everyone else was gone. She had to talk to him.

"Bless me, Father, for I have sinned, it's been a week since my last confession. Patrick, it's me, Lupe. I have to tell you something." Lupe started to cry.

"What is it, lass? Why have you been so distant?"

"I'm...I'm going to have a baby—your baby." Lupe felt herself being lifted from the kneeler and taken onto Patrick's lap on the priest's side of the confessional.

"Lupe, that's wonderful. It's a sign—God wants us to be together." He hugged her close. "I love you—marry me."

"But you're a priest. You can't get married." Lucy sobbed into his chest.

"I won't be a priest anymore. I don't want to be a priest. Let's leave Morenci and start a new life somewhere else."

"But my parents..."

"We won't tell them, until we get to where we're going." He pulled out his handkerchief and wiped her face with it. "I'll think about where to go tonight. Tomorrow, meet me here in the church at five o'clock. Bring a small suitcase with just a few things in it." He kissed her. "Remember, I love you!"

Lupe walked home in the dark. Maybe things had worked out for the best. She loved Patrick so much. Now she could be with him.

The next day did not go fast enough for Lupe. A little before five, she told her mother she was going to Tillie's and left the house. *Madre de Dios*, please forgive her for the lie. She hated to leave her parents without saying goodbye but it was the only way. She couldn't face them with the truth. Just before she got to the church, Lupe retrieved her suitcase from a thicket of bushes where she had hidden it on her way to early Mass that same morning.

Lupe entered the dark, empty church, her footsteps echoing on the wooden floor. "Patrick?" He wasn't there yet. She sat on the nearest pew to wait and studied the stained-glass window of Saint Theresa. How many times had she looked at it, thinking that some day she would wear the same veil? Now her life had taken a different turn.

Lupe glanced at her watch. Five-thirty. Where was Patrick? She looked around the church and the statue of *la Virgen de Guadalupe* caught her eye. Light from the votive candles below lit its face. Something glistened on its cheeks. Tears? Tears sprang to her own eyes as she realized Patrick wasn't coming. Dazed, she stood up and stumbled out of the church.

The following Sunday, Father Maloney announced from the lectern that Father Patrick O'Donnell had been transferred to another parish. Lupe had already resigned herself to life without Patrick. It seemed as if all the color had gone out of her life with his departure. What would she do? She couldn't even decide what to wear in the morning, much less figure out a plan.

Several days later, Tillie knocked at the Santos' door. She was carrying a large paper bag. "Come on, kiddo. We're going to the ruins." Tillie pulled Lupe out of the house. "We have to talk."

She didn't let go of Lupe's arm until they got to the old concentrator ruins. They had played there as children and as teen-agers, shared their most intimate secrets with each other.

"Sit!" Tillie pointed to the block of concrete that overlooked the football field below. She plopped down beside her. In the distance, sulfur smoke rose up from the active smelter. "Now tell me what's going on with you, Miss High Cheekbones. I'm off to the University in a couple of days, but I can't leave you in this condition."

"It's nothing. I'm okay."

"You call not eating okay? Not smiling—not talking? You're not okay. Are you having second thoughts about the convent?"

"It's not that... I'm just tired all the time."

"Come on, Lupe. You're just a ghost of yourself—something is wrong. Spill it! Maybe I can help. I always have, you know." She beamed a puckish grin.

"Oh, Tillie—everything is wrong!" Lupe blurted out, and turned to her friend. "I'm pregnant and I don't know what to do. My life is ruined." She started crying.

"It's okay. I'm here." Tillie wrapped her arms around Lupe and patted her back. "Why didn't you say so in the first place? It happens to the best of us. See down there?" She pointed to New Town, a collection of ramshackle houses clinging to the hill below. "A woman lives there who can do something about it. I'll take you to her."

"No! No, I can't do that." Lupe pulled away. "You don't understand—this is Patrick's baby."

"Father Pat? You and Father Pat? I saw the way you looked at each other and I thought something was going on. Lupe, why didn't you tell me?"

"We only did it once—that time I took my jazz records to his house. I felt so bad about it afterwards that I stayed away from him." Lupe wrung her hands. "When I figured out I was pregnant, I told him. We planned to run away together and get married except he never showed up and... and then Father Maloney said he was transferred. I don't know where he is."

Tillie was lost in thought. "Didn't you tell me that Sister Socorro's convent was connected to a home for unwed mothers?"

"Yeah—the nuns house the girls until they give birth, then find people to adopt the babies."

"That's it!" Tillie snapped her fingers. "You go to Oklahoma City next month just as planned, but instead of the convent—you go to the home. You can leave Morenci and no one will ever know."

"But what about the convent? They'll know I'm an unwed mother and they won't accept me into the order."

"Sure they will. Remember Sister Clara this summer? She told us she was married for twenty years and they let her become a nun after her husband died. She had two kids." Tillie smiled and patted Lupe's arm. "They'll take you—don't worry."

"Maybe this plan will work—I should have told you my problem earlier! Thank you." Lupe kissed Tillie's cheek. "I was so scared, I couldn't think straight."

"You've got less than a month before you leave. Cheer up—start eating right—otherwise your parents are going to get suspicious." Tillie reached into her bag and opened a lumpy foil packet filled with chocolate chip cookies.

The day before Lupe was scheduled to leave for Oklahoma City, she went out to the ruins again as she had every afternoon since Tillie left for college. It was a clear, crisp October day. The "suffer smoke" spewed out of the smokestack below, but it was drifting away from Morenci. Lupe sat on the cement block. She was grateful Tillie had brought her here a few weeks ago and helped her figure out a plan. Her parents were so proud she was going into the convent; they'd have been devastated to learn she was pregnant. This way they would never have to find out. The baby would go to a good

Catholic home and she could still become a nun. A shadow fell over Lupe and she looked up.

"Patrick! What are you doing here?"

"I came to get you, lass." He hugged her and kissed away her tears.

"Get me? You left and I..." Patrick covered her lips with his fingers.

"I have a lot of explaining to do—I know. Father Maloney had me transferred, and it happened so fast I couldn't call you. It happened right after Mass that last Sunday I was supposed to meet you." Patrick lifted her hand up to his lips and kissed it. "He told me he was tired of having so many girls confessing to impure thoughts about me—he wanted me out of here before something happened. The housekeeper packed all my things and Father drove me to Tucson to the retreat center."

Patrick explained how he had spent a miserable few days in retreat and finally told the priests he wanted out of the priesthood. "I went to Phoenix. I figured I could get a job and a place for us. It wasn't as easy as I thought—that's why I didn't come for you sooner."

"But why didn't you call? I was miserable. I didn't know what to do."

"I'm sorry. I wanted to prove to myself I could make it outside the priesthood. I didn't want to give you false hope."

"I would have gone with you whether you had a job or not." Lupe squeezed his hand.

"While I was in retreat, I realized I couldn't take you out of your home without having a job and somewhere to take you." He smoothed back a strand of hair from Lupe's face. "Anyway, now I have both. I'm working as a draft counselor and I've rented us a small house near the university—you'll like it. It's in an area where ex-priests and ex-nuns have settled. They're all working in various ways to end the war in Vietnam."

Patrick stood and pulled Lupe against him. His muscular arms enveloped her and Lupe recalled the day she had wrapped his cossack around herself and wished it were him.

"I love you, Lupe, and I want you to be my wife." He tilted her face up to his and kissed her before she had a chance to tell him how much she loved him also.

"Come on." Patrick gave her his hand. "Let's go tell your parents."

"My parents? Oh, no—we can't. They'll die. No—let's just leave without telling them."

"Lupe, we have to tell them. I can't take you without letting them know where you are."

"They'll never forgive me for this. I know they'll disown me. They'll be so ashamed of me. Please, Patrick, can't we just go?"

"No. We can't start off our new life that way. I want them to know how much I love you and assure them I'll take care of you the rest of your life."

Lupe allowed herself to be led down a dirt path to her home. Her heart was in her throat. Patrick was right. Her parents loved her and had a right to know.

"Ah, *Padre*, so you found our Lupita." Her father was sitting at the kitchen table drinking coffee. "Come—sit down—have some coffee. Tomorrow, Lupita, she goes to the convent."

"*Señor* and *Señora* Santos, we have something to tell you." Patrick sat across from her father and accepted a steaming cup of coffee. "Lupe and I are in love—we're going to be married."

"No—how can that be?" Lupe's mother covered her ears and kept shaking her head. "No...you are a priest. Lupita is going to be a nun. This cannot be happening."

"What are you saying? You cannot marry our daughter." He grabbed his daughter's hand. "Is this some kind of joke? This is not funny, Lupita."

"It's not a joke, *Papá*. I love Patrick and we're going to get married."

"How can you do this, Lupe? You've always been so religious—how can you steal a priest from his vocation?" Lupe's mother wiped her eyes with her apron.

"She's not stealing me away. I left the priesthood last month. I have a job in Phoenix and that's where we're going to live."

"No!" Her father stood up, knocking over the chair he had been sitting on. "No! This is not right. Lupe may not go with you. I forbid it." He slammed his fist on the table. "Go to your room, Lupe. Father O'Donnell, I ask you politely to leave our home."

"*Papá*, I'm leaving with Patrick. I'm pregnant—we want to get married."

"No—this cannot be. *Virgen Santísima...*" Her mother crumpled to the floor.

Lupe's father rushed to her. "Get out—the both of you—get out." He pointed to the door. "You have brought shame to the Santos' family, Lupe. I never want to see you again."

He cradled his wife's head, trying to revive her. Lupe went to the sink for water. "No, I will take care of her—you leave."

Patrick took Lupe's arm. "Go get your things. I'll wait for you on the porch."

Lupe sobbed as she ran to her room. She grabbed the suitcase she had packed to take to the convent and went back through the kitchen. Neither one of her parents looked at her. There was an ache in her heart—a void. Her father had never spoken to her like that. She went out the door and Patrick took the valise from her. He pulled her away from the house.

"I can't leave like this."

"There's no other way. They've had a shock. Let's give them time to get over it and we'll call them. One thing I learned from being a priest in this parish—Mexican families never disown their children." He helped Lupe into a car at the bottom of the hill. "They'll come around—you'll see."

As they drove through Morenci, Lupe looked at the town for the last time. More houses had been torn down. Tillie was probably right—soon the whole town would be gone. She rested her hand on Patrick's arm and smiled at him through her tears.

The next morning, Father Maloney unlocked the church and turned on the lights. He looked at the altar of *la Virgen de Guadalupe* as he did every morning since Lourdes Delgado had discovered tears on the statue's cheeks. The statue was not there! The priest sprinted up the aisle and found it at the foot of the altar. It was split in half from crown to toe. On each side of her face, twin streams of tears ran down *la Virgen's* cheeks. Father Maloney reached down and touched them. He brought the wetness up to his mouth and tasted. It was salty! The rest of the statue was dry.

¡Madre de Dios! Maybe as *Señora* Delgado had said—it was a miracle. He picked up the statue and propped it against the altar rail. As he was considering what to do next, he heard the *señora* behind him.

"*¡Es un milagro!*" *Señora* Delgado hobbled to the back of the church before Father Maloney could stop her. She tugged on the bell rope and the rich tone of the bell pealed out over Morenci, calling its people to the church.

Father Maloney was deep in thought. A miracle—that's what was needed to save the town. Maybe *la Virgen de Guadalupe* had just provided it.

Printed in the United States
894900002B